Something Unexpected

Tressie Lockwood

Sugar and Spice Press

Something Unexpected
Tressie Lockwood

All rights reserved.

Copyright © November 2010 Tressie Lockwood
Cover Art Copyright © November 2010 Anastasia Rabiyah

This is a work of fiction. All characters and events portrayed in this novel are fictitious or used fictitiously. All rights reserved, including the right to reproduce this book, or portions thereof, in any form.

Publisher:
Sugar and Spice Press
North Carolina, USA
www.sugarnspicepress.com

Something Unexpected

Chapter One

"What's she got that I don't have?" Zacari looked down at her chest. Thirty-six C bra size, a sexy if not flat belly, and a round booty men liked to grab onto even when she hadn't given them permission. She completed a two year college degree and was struggling through to bachelors. One couldn't call her glorified secretarial position success, but damn it, she supported the top executives at Connor and O'Connor, her engineering firm. That had to count to count for something, didn't it?

No, with all she had going for her, Zacari's best friend had still stolen her man and slept with him in Zacari's bed. Okay, so common sense told her the two of them were the bastards since they'd done the cheating. Knowing that didn't make Zacari feel any better about herself.

She lifted the glass of sex-on-the-beach to her lips and took a long drink. Usually she'd instruct the bartender to go easy on the alcohol and give her more orange juice, but tonight she'd begged for the booze—anything to drown her sorrows.

Zacari drained the glass and ordered anther drink. She tried to recall a drink strong enough to put her in an alcohol-induced coma, but Pam had always been the drink expert. Every time they went out, Pam would advise Zacari on what to order, and Zacari would follow along. She'd have to stick with frou frou ones now.

By the end of the fourth glass, the bartender seemed to be evaluating whether he should give her more. The room dipped and swayed each time Zacari turned her head. She sat up straight and held the side of the bar in a death grip in an effort to look sober.

"Um…" she said too loud.

The bartender glanced her way and shook his head. "I think you've had enough, miss. How are you getting home?"

She frowned. "I've only had four. My friend can drink that much with no affects whatsoever, and she can draw every man in the vicinity too." Aware she sounded resentful, Zacari clicked her teeth together. Somewhere in her past, she remembered hearing that silence made the idiot seem wise. Now that she was good and sloshed, mentally quoting proverbs like that would help. *Not!*

A male arm reached around her and set cash on the bar. "I'll take care of her tab and see her home."

Zacari gave a slow heavy-lidded blink and peered at the man. Sexy as hell, his eyes were aqua green in sharp contrast to his raven dark hair. He parted full lips in a gentle smile. For the life of Zacari she couldn't place where she'd seen him before. Surely, a guy this hot should have burned an imprint into her memory.

The bartender's brows creased. "I will call her a cab." He probably figured the man was going to rape her in some back alley and leave her dead. She should be more alarmed at the prospect, but her mind remained fuzzy. Yeah, she couldn't hold her liquor for crap.

"Zacari, let's go." The man took her arm. Had she mentioned her name?

He led her out of the bar and over to the curb. A limo pulled up as if expecting them, and the driver hopped out to open the door. Zacari resisted the hand at her lower back directing her to get in. Although it wasn't likely a man would kidnap a woman with such an obvious vehicle, she wasn't taking any chances. People were crazy. Besides, the chilly evening air cleared her head somewhat, and she was able to put more than two thoughts together.

She pulled away from his touch. "What's going on here? Why is someone like you being so nice to me?"

He stared into her eyes, amusement clear in his expression. "You don't know do you?"

"Know what?" Zacari wasn't admitting anything. If he thought he could force himself on her without a fight, he had another thought coming. He would walk away with that pretty boy face scratched to ribbons. Suffusing that threat into her stance and expression didn't wipe the grin from his full lips—lips she wanted to suck on. Zacari shook her head. Alcohol must still be clouding her judgment.

"I know that we've only met twice before, but I liked to think that I made an impression on you." He shoved his hands into his pockets. Broad shoulders fit well in his suit jacket. He paused a beat for her response, but when she didn't say a word, he continued. "I am Jack O'Connor's son. You really know how to shrink a man's ego."

Zacari's mouth fell open. Of course. That's where she'd seen the eyes, but with wrinkles all around them and saggy lids. She'd always thought when the president of her company was young, he must have been handsome. His hair all white may have been as dark as this man's at one time.

"Keary O'Connor," she said after some time.

"Ah, redeemed. Yes, that's me. Now, can I see you home?" He stepped aside to let her climb into the limo, and Zacari complied this time.

Inside, she sat well away from him with her arms crossed over her chest. While she knew her boss couldn't fault her for the formfitting dress or being out late, needing his son to take her home looked bad.

Keary sat in silence at her side until Zacari realized he waited for her address. She blushed. "Sorry, it's been a long day." She gave him the information and advised him on the direction to take.

His eyebrows went up. "So far from home."

She looked away. "I didn't want to run into anyone I knew." Meaning her ex-boyfriend and her ex-best friend, of course. Who knew she'd still have bad luck and land where she didn't want to be.

Zacari eyed Keary. Damn, he was fine. His casual slacks hugged muscular thighs, and the jacket and dress shirt didn't begin to hide his hard body. She bet his girlfriend wouldn't think twice about another man if she had Keary to come home to every day.

The lust must have been reflected in her eyes, because Keary studied her with interest. She didn't know what made her do it, but she reached out a hand and rested it on his arm. With no conscious thought, she ran her fingers up his sleeve to take a few strands of his silky hair in between her fingers. Zacari had never slept with a white man before, but she'd fantasized about it often enough. Something about their colorful eyes made her want to stare into them while running her fingers through their hair.

Maybe it was the alcohol in her system or because she was on the rebound, all her inhibitions melted away. She pulled her feet out of her heels and slid closer to Keary. When her hip brushed his, she moved one leg over his, feeling the muscles tense and bunch under her thigh.

Meeting his heated gaze, she reached between his legs and began stroking his cock. Keary covered her hand, but his shaft still jerked and hardened. "You shouldn't do that," he told her.

She smirked. "Why? You don't like it?"

He shook his head. "You know good and well that I like it. *A lot.* But I don't want to take advantage of you."

"Who is taking advantage of whom?" She pushed his hand away and traced his length through his slacks. The girth alone must be a figment of her imagination. She couldn't wait to have a closer look, but she needed him to agree. "You're not into black women?"

"That's not it at all." He lifted her hand from his crotch and kissed it. "You know how beautiful you are. There can't be a man within yards of you who will not appreciate your incredible curves, those luscious breasts, or long to taste your smooth chocolate skin."

Zacari warmed all over at his compliments, but she wasn't taking no for an answer. She was a big girl and knew what she was getting herself into. Okay, so her heart hurt like hell, but she didn't think she'd regret anything that happened tonight.

"Let me be upfront with you, Keary. I was back there drinking myself silly because I walked into my apartment and found my boyfriend getting it on with my best friend. Neither of those bastards were sorry, and I don't know how long it had been going on. I just wanted to forget it all for one night."

His beautiful eyes filled with sympathy, and he murmured those same sentiments. She was determined to change that expression. At her nape, she untied and let fall the spaghetti straps which did little to hold back her breasts. Keary followed her movements with his eyes.

"I'm on the rebound. I admit that, but I'm not the kind of woman that has these experiences every day."

"Oh? What kind of experience is that?"

She climbed onto his lap and hiked her short dress even higher. Arching her back, she pressed her breasts against his chest and was rewarded with his twitching cock under her. "This kind—having sex in a limo with a hot man."

Still Keary hesitated. He appeared to be everything a woman could want in a man. Too bad this was not the time to develop a deeper relationship.

"Since we're being honest, let me say that I've never been with a black woman, although like most men, I've fantasized about it. I would not want to take advantage of you in this vulnerable state just to fulfill it." He shuddered when she rotated her hips on his lap. "That's not to say that you're not driving me insane doing that, Zacari. A man can only take so much."

"Then don't take it." She leaned in and brushed his

lips with hers. "Or do."

Keary stared into her eyes a moment. She could almost see the wheels turning, him analyzing what was the right thing to do. If Zacari was a little more sober, maybe she'd have done the same, but why should she? His chest under her palms was solid and strong. His heart raced. Just knowing she'd excited him was a thrill in itself, and if they were a sexual match, then she was in for real ride.

Coming to a decision, Keary peered around her and tapped on the divider separating them from the driver. The barrier lowered an inch. "Sir?"

"Drive around for a while," Keary instructed. His employee didn't question him but obeyed.

Tossing Keary a sexy grin, Zacari reached back and unzipped her dress. The silky material slipped lower, and Keary drew in a sharp breath as her nipples came into view. She hadn't worn a bra since even a strapless one would have been uncomfortable in her tight outfit.

She ran her hands over her taut nipples, plucked them, and raised a questioning eyebrow to Keary. "Do you like them?"

"Hell, yes," he growled. "Play with them for me."

She pinched her nipples and stroked her breasts, allowing the peaks to graze her palms. Her lids grew heavy, and she tilted her head back knowing he didn't miss a movement. The limo hit a bump sending Zacari gently up and then down on Keary's cock. He swore, his hands moving to her hips and his fingers tangling in the waist band of her panties. When he tugged downward, Zacari helped him remove them before settling in place again.

"Let me taste," he demanded.

He explored her lips with his at first, sticking his tongue into her mouth. Zacari moaned. She invited him in, amazed at how great a kisser he was. But Keary seemed to crave more. His kisses led lower to her neck and down farther to her breast. He took one nipple into his mouth and sucked hard. Zacari cried out. She grasped his shoulder and arched more into him. Arrows of need shot to her pussy.

"Oh, baby, you're going to make me come, and we've barely started," she murmured.

"Trust me," he assured her, "you'll come more than once before I'm done."

He made good on his promise when he found her clit, stroked it with the pad of one thumb, and didn't let up until she her core muscles tightened, her body screaming for release. She bent back, bracing a hand on his knee. While his tongue drove her nuts laving her nipple, he kept up a steady pace massaging her clit. Zacari pumped against his hand begging him not to stop. Her orgasm came with sudden force making her jerk and cry out. Keary didn't pause until she'd keened through several aftershocks, and still she wanted more.

She slid to the end of his thighs and began working his belt open. Keary sat back allowing her to unbutton and unzip his slacks before reaching inside his boxers. Zacari bit down on her lip at his sheer size. So thick and hard, his cock jutted out from his body ready to satisfy the need her orgasm hadn't quieted.

Rather than take him right in, Zacari decided to give back a little of the pleasure he'd given her. She slipped from his lap and laid out across the seat. When her mouth was on a level with his cock, she peered up at him while she took the head between her lips. Keary's breath hissed past his teeth. Zacari guided him farther, angling her head so she could deep throat him.

Keary's jaw muscle contracted. "How did you learn to do that? Damn, it feels good. Baby, you're going to make me spill in your mouth."

She drew back. "And that's a bad thing?"

"Woman, you are incredible!"

She laughed and then went back to concentrating on his shaft. From his balls to his head, she licked, savoring every inch. She squeezed as she stroked, sucked at the top, and then tongued his opening. When Zacari reached down to massage his balls, they tightened. Knowing he was about to explode, she took him deep again but kept playing with the sensitive skin at his sack.

Keary knotted his fingers in her hair. He drove her down just enough so she took another inch, but not enough to hurt. One barked warning preceded his eruption, and her mouth filled with his hot come. Zacari took every drop, drinking him down and loving the flavor.

When she finished, she sat up but took hold of his cock again. Keary pulled her hand away and crooked a finger at her. "Come here."

She cast him an innocent look. "What?"

"On your knees, beautiful woman."

She smiled. "You're not ready yet."

"You think not?" He grasped her hand and placed it on his cock. In her palm, it grew out, swelling and stiffening. Zacari's mouth watered all over again, but Keary flipped her to her belly. He hoisted her onto her knees. The roominess of the limo made it easy to stretch across the black leather seats.

Keary pushed his pants and boxers lower. Her dress was now a strip around her middle while her breasts and ass were bare. Zacari purred when Keary fingered her anus. He pressed his other hand on her back, making her lean lower so her rear punctuated the air and opened her pussy wide.

Hoping he'd be a rough lover, just as she liked it, she steadied herself at the door. Keary positioned his cock at her sex and rubbed the head in her flowing cream. Zacari closed her eyes moaning. She couldn't wait until he pushed in. Having to stretch her mouth wide to take him in, she knew he'd force her pussy to expand around his girth.

The domical head parted her folds and pierced her entrance. Zacari shuddered. At first she tensed, but then Keary stroked her ass. "Easy, baby. Relax for me."

Zacari reached down between her legs and felt for his cock. She let the smooth surface glide over her fingers as Keary pushed into her. Moaning, she willed her muscles to loosen. "You're so big, Keary, so long. I want all of it. Push it in. Feels so good."

Her lover began a slow grind, arching his hips with each thrust. Zacari shoved back and gasped at how much he stretched her, how full she felt. They increased the pace until he slammed into her pussy. She had to put both hands back on the door to keep from flying forward.

"You like it hard, Zacari?" he demanded.

"Yes! Harder, please!"

His fingers dug into her hips, and he pounded deep. His control was so excellent that he didn't bang into her cervix or hurt her too much. The smallest pain coupled with unadulterated bliss made her bite back a scream. Another orgasm pulsed through her system. She leaned on an elbow and twisted back to see him. Keary's intense expression showed how much he enjoyed every plunge. He caught her watching him smacked her ass. She whimpered, but he soothed away the sting.

Their gazes locked. Keary slowed his pace and squeezed her hip. When he laid down over her, he cupped one of her breasts and captured her lips in a kiss. With their tongues curling together and them hungrily tasting each other, Zacari whimpered through another orgasm. Keary tensed with his second release.

Both trying to catch their breath, they settled together with Zacari in Keary's arms. For those brief moments, Zacari forgot what happened earlier, and she'd had the best sex of her life.

"Thank you," she whispered.

Keary yawned. She giggled knowing men liked to fall asleep after they'd been satisfied.

"For what?"

She lifted his hand to her mouth and kissed the back of it. "For making me forget and showing me a good time."

Chapter Two

Zacari woke up on the couch in her living room. For a minute she couldn't remember why the heck she was out here, but then it all came flooding back. Her jerk of an ex had cheated in her bed. She hadn't even been in there since she discovered it.

As she sat up, her head began to spin. She winced and sucked in a couple of deep breaths. If she'd had the good sense to have dinner last night before drinking, she wouldn't be this sick. Swinging her feet over the edge of the couch, she recalled something else. Keary.

The back of Zacari's hand flew to her mouth. "Oh goodness, I can't believe I did that. I seduced my boss's son." She so did not need to drink—*ever again*.

On the other hand, it had been good, *really* good. The fact that she was sore between her legs was a testament to that. She remembered asking her boyfriend to give it to her rough like Keary did, but he'd been too weak or disinterested. But Keary? Oh man, she could not regret the decision to seduce that boy. He was hot as hell.

Grinning from ear to ear, Zacari paused when a sound

from her bedroom reached her. The door was closed, but someone was in there. The alarm clock had just gone off, followed by a male grunt and a slam she assumed was him hitting the snooze button.

"Oh hell no," she muttered. That cheating ass was still here. She didn't know why she'd thought otherwise. His name was on the lease just like hers, and just like her he had no family he could stay with.

Why he didn't go stay at her friend's house, she didn't know, but Zacari wasn't sticking around to find out. She'd spend this weekend looking for somewhere else to live. The next time she laid eyes on that bastard, she hoped it would be at his funeral.

Zacari tiptoed around the apartment looking for the duffle bag she knew was there. She found it and waited for her ex to get in the shower before she hurried into her bedroom and stuffed a few needed items into the bag. After he was gone, she'd come back for the rest. With her toothbrush and other essential toiletries in hand, she dropped the bag by the front door and headed across the hall to her neighbor's place.

Melvin, her ex, was what some called a metrosexual male. Zacari knew he'd be in the bathroom a good hour, maybe longer. She could shower, dress, and be gone before he ever knew she'd been there. With some lame excuse about calling maintenance about her plumbing, she convinced her neighbor to let her use the shower, and then Zacari was on her way.

She caught a taxi downtown to retrieve her car at the bar and then ran across the street to a coffeehouse where she could nurse the pain in her head with caffeine and look in the paper for rentals. Something month-to-month would be perfect for now. Within an hour, she found what she was looking for and dialed the number on her cell.

"Hi, is this Richardson Rental Properties?" she asked when a woman answered mumbling something incomprehensible.

"Yes, it is," the woman sang too cheery.

"I understand you have month-to-month. Can I come in there today and move in on tomorrow or Monday? Do you have a unit ready?"

"Wow, sweetie we'd need to check your references and things—"

"What if I give you three months rent up front plus security?" Zacari crossed her fingers under the table and cringed at having to dip into her savings, but she had no choice. She'd call her current apartment manager and tell him what was happening. Hopefully, he'd understand.

"Let me ask my manager. Hold on."

Zacari waited. She deliberately called one of the hotel converted to apartments places having heard that they would cut a deal with just about anybody. As long as she had the cash, they didn't care. She hoped that still held true.

The woman came back on the line. "Okay, sweetie, if you can get here before we close with the cash, you can move in on Monday."

"Not tomorrow?"

"Sorry, Monday's the earliest. Is that okay?"

"Yes, that's fine." She wrapped up the call and slumped in her chair cradling her coffee. All of a sudden, when she'd thought her life was in perfect order, she was slung into chaos. Worse, for two days, she'd be homeless. Zacari prepared to accept what she couldn't change. Her mother might have died when Zacari was twelve, but in the little time she'd known her, her mother had taught her to be strong and independent. One way or another everything would work out.

* * * *

Zacari snatched her note pad off her desk, fiddled with the run in her pantyhose, and hurried to make a meeting on time. From the first step into the conference room, she couldn't take her eyes off Jack O'Connor—that is until he looked back at her. Then everything in the room was more interesting than him. Did he know she'd had sex with his son Friday night, probably in a car he used? When she thought of it that way, it seemed so sleazy.

Saying nothing, she slipped into a seat as far away from Jack as possible. The notepad clutched between numb fingers became her focal point, a safe haven. This was ridiculous of course. She wasn't a child, and neither was Keary. She could chant those facts over and over, but the flutters in her stomach didn't care.

"Zacari, is there a problem?"

Her mouth went dry at Jack's question, but she straightened and cleared her throat. "Oh, no problem. Just have a lot on my mind this morning."

Jack's friendly smile unsettled her more. Everyone spoke of how personable he seemed. Jack had a trick he used to remember all the employees' names, from the clerk in the mailroom to the seasonal temps. The day she met him and he laid his hand on her shoulder offering that same smile had warmed her and made her glad to be a part of his vision for Connor and O'Connor.

"Good," Jack said, "I'm glad to hear it. I know you were out yesterday, but I wanted to bring you up to speed on the changes taking place at C-O-C." That was Jack treating her like an executive and not just an assistant.

"Cock," someone coughed followed by a few titters. That joke was getting old. Jack liked to shorten the company name to initials, but many called it Cock instead. It had been funny the first half a dozen times.

"As you know, Zacari," Jack said, ignoring the joke, "and everyone else, we're having some issues in our branch in Cairo right now. A few fires, nothing we can't handle. I sent my son Keary to take care of it—"

"Keary?" Zacari almost shouted, and everyone turned to look at her. She cleared her throat and tugged on her hair before lowering her eyes. "I mean, go on."

Jack chuckled. "Yes, Keary. Trust me, if there's anything to be done, he'll do it. I know how people think just because a man owns a large corporation, he places his incompetent children in positions of authority. No way! I spent a fortune on Keary's education and training. He can handle Cairo."

Zacari found it odd that the original Connor who had begun the corporation was just a name. No one had ever seen him, but then the rumor was that he had the money to begin the venture, but Jack had the brains. The other man seemed to be happy with the fact that his name came first and he collected a huge paycheck.

"That's what I like about you, Jack," one of the VP's cut in, "you shoot from the hip. You're right up front in addressing the real issues, and you don't pull punches."

"Yeah, just like he 'punched' you out last week for

that software flub," another man teased.

The VP reddened, but Jack wrenched control of the conversation again and continued his report. Zacari's thoughts were no longer on the meeting. She couldn't help thinking of Keary. They'd made no plans to see each other again. In fact, she'd made sure to hop out of the limo when it pulled up to her place, and with nothing more than a wave and a "it was amazing" tossed over her shoulder, she'd disappeared inside.

Zacari didn't indulge in one night stands, but that's all Friday night was. What she needed to do now was put it behind her. If she revisited the night in her thoughts, it should be to enjoy the fact that she'd seduced a sexy rich dude and leave it there. Besides, Jack didn't behave like he knew anything, and from what she knew of the Cairo mess, Keary would be gone a while. So no awkwardness at work—*bonus!*

By the end of the day, Zacari was much more relaxed and feeling positive. She'd spent the night in her car on Sunday which wasn't so bad since the warm weather held. Now she was moved into her place. On her way out of the office, she checked her watch. On Tuesday after work, Melvin hit the gym. This was a perfect opportunity to slip into the apartment and grab the rest of her stuff.

She found her car in the company parking lot and headed out. Fifteen minutes later, she arrived and hopped out of the car. If her head wasn't filled with questions of what she'd have for dinner later, she might have noticed the purple bug. Not until she'd pushed her key into the lock and opened the door did she realize.

Pam came from the bedroom wearing a short teddy that showed off her long curvy legs. Her weave with blond streaks sat wild and sexy about her head. Even though she wasn't dressed for the day, Pam had already donned her makeup including false lashes and heavy eyeliner. Zacari knew from going with her the day she got them that Pam had piercings and tattoos that would have any man's tongue hanging out in lust.

"What are you doing here?" Pam demanded. "I thought you moved out." Her hand went to her hip. "Melvin's going to need that key back."

"Excuse me, but my name is still on the lease," Zacari informed her while she slammed the door. "Yours isn't. And I have to get the rest of my stuff."

"Well hurry up."

Zacari paused on the way to the closet. "What's with the attitude, Pam? Maybe you forgot, but I was the one wronged, not you. You were supposed to be my best friend, and we'd been through a lot together long before Melvin came on the scene."

Pam sucked her teeth and rolled her eyes. "Whatever, that's old news. He's with me now."

"Don't sound so threatened," Zacari spat. "Trust me, I don't want him back."

"As if you could get him."

Zacari sighed. "Whatever." She walked to the bedroom and opened the closet. All of her clothes had been dumped into a pile in the corner of the walk-in. What she didn't get was what all the hostility was about. Hell, she could have told them to take it somewhere else and she would keep the apartment. She'd never begged or cried demanding to know why they treated her like this. She didn't even yell or curse either of them out. Most people would have. Zacari just walked away and cried in private then attempted to drink herself silly. And here she was subjected to this crap, her stuff thrown aside like she'd done something wrong.

Pam, obviously wanting a fight, followed her into the bedroom and stood over her like Zacari tried to steal something. "See that's how you are, Zacari, a cold heartless bitch. Melvin told me how you wouldn't react when he told you stuff you didn't want to hear. You never argue or fight back. You just do what you want to do, and he has to find out later that you didn't give a damn what he did or said."

Zacari whirled on her. "And that's where you came in right, all loving support?"

Pam flipped her hair, the teddy straining over her breasts and outlining her nipples. Zacari wanted to throw up as she thought of how Melvin must have loved seeing her ex-friend like that. Pain tightened her chest. Pam was so off base thinking she didn't have a heart.

"Why not?" Pam admitted. "Melvin is a young black man going places. He's already pulling in fifty thousand a year, and he's ready to go into business with his boy. That's on the side until they make it full time. After that, he's going to blow up huge."

"So that's what it's about, the money?" Zacari went to the kitchen to grab a couple trash bags and came back to dump her stuff into it. "You're eye candy, and he pays for it with his wallet."

Pam purred. "Don't hate because I have what you messed up and lost."

Zacari stood up and gathered her things. "Trust me, it's not hating. Just like I told Melvin when he asked my opinion, this business deal is a bad move. He's going to get burned. I keep my ears open at work, and I learn a lot. In school I'm taking tons of business classes. I know what I'm talking about."

"You are a secretary, Zacari, and you only have your Associates degree. What do you know?"

"I may be an *assistant*, but that doesn't make me an idiot. Melvin doesn't have a degree, and he got where he is riding his uncle's coattails. If you think that qualifies him to know business, you're the fool. Maybe you're right. Maybe I wasn't as supportive as I could have been, but I'm out of it now. You can save the attitude for someone else. You won't be seeing me again."

With that, Zacari headed down to her car. Behind the wheel, she slipped on sunglasses and blinked away the moisture in her eyes before pulling off. Pam had been so wrong about how she felt. Sure she didn't let people see her cry very often, but that didn't mean she had no feelings. And so what she was independent and strong. There was nothing wrong with that. Melvin should have been man enough to break up with her if he wasn't happy not sneak around behind her back, and it was for damn sure he wasn't with Pam because she was the sweet supportive wife type. Pam represented slutty sex, nothing more, and by her own admission, she just wanted Melvin's money. Well, he would learn. Zacari had every intention of moving on.

Chapter Three

Three weeks later

Zacari glanced up at the mirror over her bathroom sink and grinned. A promotion and relocation couldn't have come at a better time. Twice in her big ass city, she'd spotted Pam and Melvin together. Once they'd been shopping at the mall in a furniture store, and another time, she'd seen them downtown on the street. Both instances, Melvin pretended he didn't see Zacari, and Pam cast her triumphant looks without shame. Why couldn't the girl just move on and be happy with what she had? Why'd she have to act like she could only have something good if it spited someone else?

"I don't care," Zacari chanted and wiped the steamed over mirror. Jack had personally told her about the new opportunity. She would have a step up in position, not exactly defined, but more money and she wasn't answering phones all day—at least not for everybody. That alone was a reason to celebrate. The executive she reported to answered his own calls. On top of everything else, she was moving to Chicago.

Still bubbling with excitement, she left the bathroom and headed to the kitchen to get a cup of coffee. Passing the calendar on the wall, she paused, and her heart felt like it hammered in her throat. *Today is the twenty-third? No, it can't be. Please, no!*

Her period came like clockwork with a half week of headaches and crankiness to warn of its arrival. Yet, she realized that it was late by several days. "Don't panic," she told herself while she flipped to the previous month. She counted out the days two and then three times. The breath she blew out seemed to whistle in her tightened chest. "Okay...panic."

Zacari didn't waste a minute debating what to do. She hightailed it over to the drug store and bought three different brands of pregnancy tests. None she'd chosen required the first pee of the day, so she got right to it. Within a few minutes the horror of her situation hit her hard, and she sank onto the bathroom floor crying her eyes out.

A thought occurred to her. Was this even Melvin's baby? Like before when she'd been calculating the date of her last period and when she should have expected it this time, she thought back to the date she'd last been with Melvin. It had been at least four or five weeks before they broke up. Hell, now that she thought of it Melvin had a high sex drive, and for him not feel in the mood said he'd already been cheating. That meant her baby's father was no one other than Keary.

What had she done? *Why* had she done it? She didn't know Keary like that. He could have been sleeping with half the female population for all she knew, which meant she could have picked up something. On top of that dumbness having no condom, she wasn't on the pill because her system went psycho when she did. The worse thing about it all was this was all her fault. Keary hadn't seduced her. She'd seduced him, had refused to take no for an answer. Now, with her irresponsibility, he was going to be a father.

For an instant, Zacari considered not telling him, but that was wrong. Keary had a right to know. She'd just make it clear that she didn't expect one thing from him. She didn't make a whole lot of money, but since the raise, there was no reason she couldn't support herself and her baby. And C-O-C health insurance was top notch. Jack had made sure of that.

Calmer now, she stood up and wiped her face. The first move she needed to make was to find out Keary's address. At her office, she had access to everyone's personal information being that she worked for the executives. She hoped it wasn't a breech of privacy since it wasn't like she wanted to stalk the man. All Zacari wanted to do was send a letter to Keary. He'd get it when he returned to the U.S., and then he could either ignore her or come find her and talk it out. Just like Zacari had access, so did Keary.

Her plans made, Zacari went about preparing to move to Chicago. Out-of-control emotions, which she attributed to being psychological, had her crying often. Zacari went through the motions of her transition coupled with changes in her body. Over the next six months, all she felt she did was vomit and moan because she *felt* like vomiting.

* * * *

Keary slung his suit bag over his shoulder and took hold of the other case by its handle. Used to travel but long past his tolerance of the desert, he was glad to be home. A low tone caught his attention, and he dug his phone out of his pocket. The message made him grin. That was the best part of getting back. He would be able to see Debbie in the Chicago office. Their relationship had been casual when he left, but over skype, it had heated up. He looked forward to seeing how much further it would go.

Of course office relationships were frowned on, but Debbie was an executive not a secretary or a clerk who others would feel he was taking advantage of. She was great in business and had an excellent head on her shoulders. Keary admired that and more. When he wanted to recall that last sexy picture she'd sent him, his mind switched to Zacari instead.

As he stepped into the waiting limo that would speed him back to his luxury apartment, he couldn't help remembering how she'd felt under him. Her body had been perfect, smooth tawny skin, curvy hips, and breasts to fit into the palms of his hands. He sighed. That had been a fling, something he would never repeat. After all, she'd been exercising some demons and getting some of her own back after her boyfriend cheated. Keary hoped he'd left her with a sigh of satisfaction the next morning rather than more regrets. He knew he didn't regret it, not for an instant. If the circumstances had been right, could he…No, he'd look like he was taking advantage of her. Keary valued his position in his father's company, and he wasn't going to give the old man or himself a bad name by going after a woman who was not at least management level. Besides, she was too sweet a woman for him to screw her over like the last asshole. Better to just move on and remember the pleasure they shared for one night.

He let himself into the apartment and tossed his keys on the hall table. Leaving his bags by the door to be unpacked later, he sifted through the piles of mail his assistant had picked up from the post office for him. Keary's eyes widened when he came to a letter from Zacari. Wondering what she had to say, he stared at the envelope rather than open it.

"You'll never know if you don't do it," he muttered.

Using a letter opener he ripped into the missive and pulled out a single hand-written sheet. He paused long enough to admire how neat her writing was. Rather than slanted like most people were taught, she wrote straight up and down. Even without guides, her lines were level rows. Having put off reading the letter long enough, Keary began at the beginning:

> Dear Keary,
>
> I want to keep this letter short and to the point. I hope you don't mind that I used my resources at work to get your address. I guess if you do, I'll find myself fired. Okay, I don't want to focus on that. I'm stalling.
>
> Listen, that night you rescued me was…amazing. I've never had it so good. I don't know if I'm puffing up your head (lol) or telling you anything you don't already know, but it worked, didn't it?
>
> Anyway, I think you have the right to

know we had a small…um…consequence to that night. Keary, oh goodness, how do I say this? I'm pregnant.

Keary sank down on the arm of the couch, staring at the letter unblinking until his eyes ached. His vision must be deceiving him. She couldn't have written what he thought, but then of course she did. Now that he thought back, he'd never used a condom. Never in his span of sexual exploits had he failed to use a condom. He didn't know her that well. Sure she had those big, pain-filled brown eyes that had drawn him in and made him not want to escape. But that didn't mean she hadn't done what they did countless times before.

Thinking that way brought up new considerations. What if this was a trap? Maybe she'd planned it all along, to get pregnant by her boyfriend and seduce him. Fuck, he'd been an idiot anyway. Keary was used to having the upper hand, but if he remembered correctly, Zacari hadn't taken no for an answer. She'd all but thrown herself on him naked. No red-blooded man could have turned that down.

Keary flung the letter aside and paced his living room while running his fingers through his hair. What was he going to do? Did she want money? How much? He guessed several thousand dollars. It wasn't like he couldn't afford it, and after all, his dick landed him in this place. He just ought to pay.

He sighed and strode back to the letter. Despite how angry he was, the feeling couldn't erase what happened that night. He was a fool and deserved this mess. After rubbing his burning eyes, he focused again on the letter.

> ...I'm pregnant. I can only imagine how angry you must be, but let me say right away that I don't expect anything from you...

Keary growled. They always said that, and then a knock sounded on the door.

> You had the right to know about the baby, but that's as far as it will go. I got a sort of promotion at work with a little more money. I'm moving to the Chicago office with Jeb, so everything will be fine.

"Chicago!" he shouted. Of all places the one office where Debbie worked ended up being where Zacari was now. No one had seen fit to inform him over the last six months that Zacari was there, but then why would they? No one knew about that night. As if Zacari sensed the direction of his thoughts, she said:

> Nobody has to know that you are my baby's father. You don't have to worry. I know this looks bad, like I set a trap for you, but I couldn't know you'd be at that bar. Then again, I guess I could have been tracking you. I'm sure there are skanks who do it. I'm not the one. In time, you'll see that's not me, when I don't come begging for money. Thank you for that night. I will remember it.
> Zacari

Keary wandered around his apartment avoiding calls and texts. When a hot shower didn't give him the solution he sought, he stepped out with pruned skin and made himself a drink. *Zacari*, his thoughts echoed over and over. She carried his baby. *His* baby. Keary hadn't planned on having kids for a while yet, and definitely with a woman he wanted to keep in his life long term.

"No use crying over it," he reminded himself. He had to face the facts, own up to his responsibility. Whether Zacari was honest or not didn't matter. Keary could not in good conscious walk away from his child. Besides, some small excitement built in him wondering what he or she would look like and how the baby's personality would develop.

At last able to think with common sense, Keary picked up the phone and made arrangements for a flight to Chicago. Whether Zacari wanted money and nothing else, Keary didn't care. She was about to get a lot more than she bargained for. Keary had every intention of being involved in his child's life one hundred percent of the time or as close as he could get to it.

He unpacked and repacked his suitcase. Within forty-five minutes, he sped toward the airport, wondering what he would find in Chicago.

* * * *

To Keary's annoyance, he couldn't arrive at the office unnoticed. He'd accessed the company's directory on the way over in order learn where Zacari sat. With that info, he'd hoped to find her and invite her to lunch so they could talk. Unfortunately, things didn't go as he planned.

"Keary! When did you get back?" Jeb pounded him on the back. "It's been a while, man. Let me take you to lunch. I'd love to hear how you single-handedly restored the Cairo branch."

Keary tightened his jaw. "Hardly."

"Don't be modest. Jack is singing your praises all over the country. At the meeting this morning, a good half of it was spent talking about all you accomplished over there."

Jeb's words held a note of bitterness. Others with more skill had tried schmoozing Keary in the past. Jeb was fooling no one. "Well if you heard it all this morning, there's nothing for me to add," he told the man, and Jeb reddened.

Keary pulled away and continued on to find Zacari. He felt he drew near to where she sat when two others called his name. Just when Keary realized it was Debbie and another manager trying to get his attention, Zacari rounded a corner with a swollen belly. Keary's eyes widened. He didn't know what he had expected, but the impact of seeing her this way did something to him he wasn't sure he should acknowledge.

The papers in Zacari's hands fluttered to the floor when she spotted him. Her full dark lips parted in a soft gasp. He found himself wanting to taste those lips.

"Keary," she murmured. He was pretty sure no one had heard her say his name.

Before he could respond to her, Debbie swooped in and hooked her arm with his. She lifted her chin almost as if she expected him to kiss her, but then she smiled. The smile said everything. "Finally, you're back," she cooed. "So we can continue our conversations in person."

Keary blinked at her. Where had the level-headed,

yet sexy, professional woman he'd been talking to gone? After considering it, Keary figured out why Debbie approached him with such open affection. If Keary was willing to date a woman from the office, then he could choose someone else as easily as he chose her. By her possessive grip on his arm, she let the entire office know he was hers.

Keary caught the knowing looks from the other men, the slaps on the back, and a whistle. He'd always enjoyed the relaxed culture in his father's company, but with this mess, he wished it was a whole lot more formal. A place where no one would dare let on that they knew what went on in his personal life. Of course if that were true, he wouldn't have considered dating a coworker in the first place.

By the time, he'd extricated himself from the crowd, Zacari was nowhere in sight. He looked like a bastard knocking her up and then pretending she didn't exist. Frustrated and inpatient to get out of there, Keary headed to an empty office with apologies to all that he had a report to get done for his father. Everyone respected Jack, so they didn't push. Keary managed to avoid saying yes to invitations and shut the office door.

This wasn't the place to have the conversation with Zacari anyway. He accessed the company's employee records and located her address. After sifting through emails the next hour, he finished up a little work. The next time he raised his head from the screen it was after five. Now was as good a time as any to face Zacari at her place. If she wasn't there, he'd wait. To his surprise, he was a lot more eager to see her than he had been to see Debbie. Who knew what would come of this meeting.

Chapter Four

Zacari tugged open the refrigerator to see what she'd have for dinner. The healthy choice would be lean meat and veggies, maybe some fruit, but what she craved was another taco with heaps of sour cream. She'd only eaten them every day for the last week.

"And my hips are carrying the evidence," she complained.

Her hips were doing more than carrying extra weight. They'd shifted making room for when the baby would be born. The movement had caused her to ache, and sleeping at night was a joke. Zacari more often tossed and turned, punched her body pillow as if it was the cause of her discomfort, and then finally fell asleep at somewhere around four a.m. All that and she still had to work full days and save as much money as possible.

She pulled out the ingredients for salad and sat down at the table with a large wooden bowl. Tearing romaine from the stalk, she paused and sighed. She wasn't hungry. Not after seeing Keary today and being ignored. He hadn't even said hi. No, he was too busy letting Debbie hang onto him. Zacari had heard what the woman said, that they'd been talking all this time, and they were going to pick up in person what they'd left off from online. So that meant they were dating.

Zacari couldn't regret telling him the truth, but by him not saying a word, she wondered if he didn't believe her. Maybe he thought she seduced men all the time and when she got pregnant tried to pin it on him because he was rich. She'd seen the movies where that junk went on. Even if it wasn't real, plenty of women could have gotten the idea from that and tried it.

She didn't blame him…much. "Who am I kidding?" She was about to pick up the bowl and throw it across the room when the doorbell rang. Zacari stopped. No one visited her. She hadn't yet made any friends being tired so much and wanting nothing more than to take a nap after work.

At the door, she looked through the peephole and froze. She took a few steps back. The baby kicked, and she rubbed her belly while still not moving. The bell rang again. "Zacari?" he called.

Longing hit her, hearing his voice. This was absurd. There'd been nothing but sex between them, and lately she couldn't even think of a cock without getting pissed off.

She opened the door. "What do you want, Keary?" Her tone had been harsher than she meant. She'd preferred to appear indifferent to him. "I thought I made it clear you have no obligation to me or the baby."

He eyed her in silence, his aqua gaze sweeping her from head to toe. When he paused at her belly, and his expression softened, she didn't know what to think. Did he want to be involved in their child's life? Was that why he'd come? Either way, she needed to calm down and hear him out. Then she'd make it clear he could walk away. She would not hold it against him.

Zacari stepped back. "Come in."

He stepped past her, and she locked the door before leading him into the living room. Zacari felt like her movements were jerky and goofy because she was nervous. Her ass had widened considerably since the last time he'd seen her, and she could only hope he wasn't staring at it while she walked.

After offering him a seat, she perched on the edge of one herself—or she would have, but perching seemed to require a lap. The baby had absorbed most of that. While she struggled to get comfortable and not look like the awkward fat cow she was, Keary leaped to his feet and rushed over to help. "Here, I've read that this helps." He tucked a throw pillow under each arm and rearranged the one she bought just for her lower back.

Her eyes widened. "Seriously? You read it?"

For a moment, he looked less like the sexy tycoon she'd ridden in his limo and more like a boy with red cheeks. Keary cleared his throat. The embarrassment was gone in an instant. "I picked up a couple of books in the airport bookstore and skimmed them on the plane. Later, when I have more time, I'll take my time and read through them."

Dumbfounded, she said, "Books on pregnant women?"

He nodded while taking his seat. "And one on caring for a newborn."

Zacari couldn't think of a word to say.

Keary leaned forward, steepling his strong hands. Zacari couldn't help thinking of those same fingers brushing over her skin, but his words brought her back to the subject at hand. "Zacari, is it too early to know what the sex of the baby is?"

"Y-You can't be interested. I said—"

"I know what you said. Now I'm saying I will be involved with my baby's life. One hundred percent involved."

One hundred percent? Against her better judgment, she began thinking about him helping her to bathe the baby, the two of them taking him for a stroll in the park, and later balling like idiots on his first day of kindergarten. Zacari shook her head and closed her eyes. No, Keary wasn't asking her to marry him, and even if he was, it was for the baby's sake. Not hers. In this day and age, parents spent time with their children even when the mother and father weren't together. They just did it separately. No big deal.

Despite how she told herself Keary being involved wasn't a problem, Zacari couldn't explain the feelings that overwhelmed her, knowing he was near. Then she thought of Debbie. "What about Debbie? It looked like you two were dating or about to start."

Zacari couldn't identify the emotions that flitted over his face. Regret? Annoyance?

"My being a part of my…"

"Son," she supplied.

His face lit up. She could almost see him passing out cigars and buying sports related clothing, and rolled her eyes.

"Being a part of my son's life has nothing to do with

Debbie. However, I think neither she nor I could have expected this. I think for right now, it's best we not start up a relationship."

Zacari frowned. "You think I expected it? I promise you, I did not set some kind of trap, and I made it crystal clear that I don't expect a dime from you. I can take care of myself and the baby. So long as Jack doesn't think I... and I lose my job and..."

"That's not going to happen," he ground out. He ran a hand through his hair and stood. "I admit I haven't thought that far ahead about letting my father know. I don't want to make it uncomfortable for you at work." He scratched the back of his neck, his beautiful eyes glazing over as he thought. "I could foot all your bills so you don't have to work."

"Oh hell no!" she shouted and struggled to her feet. Keary put out a hand, but she slapped it away. "See, that's what I knew this would lead to when you showed up at my door. No way you're taking care of me. Not now, not ever."

"Zacari, calm down," he coaxed her.

She glared at him. "I'm not some skank you made the mistake of getting pregnant and now you want to hide me away so no one knows. I don't need your money, and I don't need you." She turned to march back to the door, so she could slam it behind him on his way out, but he grabbed her hand.

With gentleness that shocked her, he pulled her back to him and rested his hand on her belly. People always thought they could touch a pregnant woman's stomach without asking. If a person couldn't put their hands on a woman any other time, pregnancy wasn't permission.

Zacari might rant and rage mentally, but she liked his touch. It calmed her and made her feel safe. Since she'd learned of her pregnancy, fears of all kinds assailed her—from whether she'd remember her little one's age to whether she would be a good mother and not be the cause of him getting therapy later in life. On top of that, she was terrified of what people would say if they knew who her son's father was, what they would think of her. Keary made all the noise in her head ease, even if for a few seconds.

"What I suggest to you," he began, "is just that—suggestions. You are free to say no and work if you like. Two things are nonnegotiable. Jack will know, and I will not walk away from my son. He will have my support financially, emotionally, and every other way a father can be there. Period."

Tremors passed through Zacari. She should move out of Keary's embrace, but she didn't want to. His warmth heated up her body, making her want so much more. Of course no man could be as wonderful as he seemed to be. Didn't he want to accuse her of lying or trapping him? She'd waited for his tirade, but instead, she got this…this gentle, considerate person that any woman would kill for, to be the father of her children. Well, she'd reserve her judgment. Everyone had flaws. Keary was just acting all sweet and wonderful. Wait until the morning when she was bitchy and everything ached but she couldn't soothe herself with a huge dose of caffeine. Then the truth would come out.

Almost chuckling, she pulled away from him. "Fine, but if Jack fires me, *you* are going to help me find another job, *not* support me."

"Deal."

"And you are not going to be overbearing acting like I can't eat tacos or something."

His eyebrows rose. "Tacos?"

"I'm just sayin'."

He grinned, making her weak all over again. "Okay, fine. But you have to eat healthy along with whatever cravings you have. And most importantly, Zacari, you must let me help you in some ways. I know you're an independent woman, and you don't want me to think you tricked me. I get that. But going so far in the opposite direction might not be the best for our son."

Her heart skipped a beat. *Get a grip*, she commanded it.

"I'm able to give him the best. If so, doesn't he deserve to enjoy the benefits of his father and grandfather's legacy?"

She put a hand on her hip. "Why does it sound like you're saying you don't want your son living in the ghetto? Or using hand-me-downs?"

"Zacari," he said in frustration. "Will you read something negative in everything I say?"

She didn't answer for a long time, battling with him in her mind but not out loud. She knew she was being unreasonable. He wanted to talk. She wanted to question his motives. Finally, she said, "How about this? We shop together if you intend to buy him something."

"And not when you do? No double standards or no deal."

Zacari sighed. "Look, I've already ruined a good thing for you with Debbie, I guess." She wasn't entirely sure Debbie was right for Keary, but whatever. He shouldn't cut her off for Zacari's sake. "There's no reason you can't still date her, and there's really nothing much to do until the baby is born. You don't have to be around until then."

"That's where you're wrong," he announced and pointed to her feet. Zacari's ankles were swollen chunks that only grew worse when she walked too much. On top of that, her feet ached.

She drew back as if he slapped her. "I'm not very attractive right now. That's what pregnancy does to you. I can't help it." *Oh crap, I'm about to cry. Damn these stupid hormones.*

Turning her back on him once again, she prepared to run out of the room until she could pull herself together, but for the second time, he stopped her. "Zacari, believe me, I wasn't criticizing how you look. You are still a beautiful and desirable woman. If it was appropriate right now, I'd *show* you."

She resisted lowering her gaze to his crotch, having the feeling that's what he meant. But that didn't prove she was still beautiful. He hadn't seen her naked. Stretch marks spidered her belly, and her thighs didn't bear glimpsing. In the shower, she avoided looking down, and the mirror was off limits beyond her neck. The only time she looked at her belly was when she had clothes on, and that was to stroke it knowing her son grew inside.

Keary placed gentle pressure on her shoulders to make her sit down, and then he took the space opposite her on the coffee table. She gasped when he pulled one leg up to rest her foot on his lap. A squeak of protest left her lips when he removed her fluffy pink slipper. "Uh-uh, don't pull away," he instructed. "I can see your feet hurt. I know this will help."

His hands felt like heaven. Her eyelids fluttered closed before she forced them up. "You shouldn't do that."

Keary ignored her. He continued to massage, from her toes, over her feet all the way up her calves. Thinking this was his way to get to her pussy, she opened her eyes, but his expression was calm not lust-filled. He worked his way down again and concentrated on the balls of her feet. This shouldn't surprise her. The condition of her body wouldn't drive anyone to desire.

"Can you enjoy it?" he asked. "Even for a moment?"

"You're reading my mind?"

He grinned at her. "I can almost feel you trying to decipher my motives. How about, whether they are good or bad, you just enjoy the pleasure. Is the ache receding? Does it feel good?"

She moaned. "You have no idea." Biting her lip, she said, "Can you do the other one?"

His eyes sparkled. "Of course."

For the next hour, Keary rubbed her feet and calves while Zacari laid back enjoying it all. She didn't care if he was trying to get on her good side, or thought doing it would help the baby. As he suggested, she just let it happen. When he was done, she curled up on the couch with a fist tucked beneath her chin. Keary watched her, the self-satisfied expression on his face amusing.

When he crouched down in front of her, she half listened to what he said as she was falling asleep. "Zacari, I'm not waiting until the baby is born to be around. I'm going to be there every step of the way from shopping for his clothes, to giving you massages or back rubs, to picking out a crib."

She yawned. "Hm, okay."

"Zacari?"

She dropped off to sleep, but just before she lost all consciousness to the world, she thought she felt Keary's lips touch her temple. Warmth spread through her system, and her final thought was that she could fall for a man like Keary seemed to be.

Chapter Five

Zacari strolled into the office with her comfort bag slung over her shoulder, a simple dress, and flats on her feet. She made a beeline for her desk, hoping to avoid anyone. Early mornings, she was grumpy as hell because she couldn't drink coffee. As soon as she sat down and powered up her computer, her phone rang. She glanced at the display and saw that it was Debbie. *Great.*

Mid-ring, the phone made another sound alerting her that a second call was coming in. Debbie's name disappeared on the display to be replaced by Jack's. Her stomach tightened, but right now, Zacari'd much rather talk to him than Debbie, so she answered.

"Hello, Jack, how are you?" She loved working in the twenty-first century when most company employees called their bosses by their first names instead of *mister* or *ms*.

"Good morning, Zacari. How's your day going so far?" While he maintained his usual pleasant tone, something told her Jack's mind was busy. Jeb was there in the office with Jack all week for meetings, so she knew he wasn't calling looking for her boss.

"It's fine so far," she answered with caution. "I just got in." Zacari quickly looked at the time on the bottom right of her computer screen. She blew out a breath. She wasn't late for a change. The last few months had been a trial. "Is there anything I can help you with? Did Jeb forget a file?"

"No." He grew quiet. Zacari felt her throat closing. "Keary told me about the baby, that it's his."

All the strength left her body. She had to hold onto the edge of the desk so she wouldn't topple sideways and land on the floor. Before she could utter a word, across the wide open space where Zacari's desk was situated, Debbie came charging out of her office with a look of irritation marring her beautiful face.

"Did you hear me calling you for the last ten minutes, Zacari!" Her voice was too loud and too shrill. Maybe she didn't see the phone line leading up to Zacari's ear, or it could have been the fact that she was pissed off and hadn't had her coffee either.

Either way, Zacari didn't appreciate the attitude. She was seconds close to snapping at Debbie to back off, when Jack spoke in her ear. "Please tell Debbie you're talking to me and you'll get back to her shortly. Let her know I need to call her later about the Shore Project."

"*Jack* says…" she began and relayed the rest of the message. The way Debbie paled, Zacari had a hard time not smirking. With a brief nod, the woman scurried back to her cave, tail firmly between her legs.

"Now about the baby," Jack continued. She could only imagine what he would say. Maybe that no son of his was going to have a baby with a black woman. Or it could be that his plan for Keary's life didn't include children out of wedlock. Zacari had always thought it was awesome how much Jack had made extra sure Keary was educated in the ways of his business and could handle anything. There was nothing wrong with that, but looked at from another perspective, Jack talked a lot about what he wanted for Keary and how he'd orchestrated this and that. Zacari was sure nothing like this was in the plan.

She'd always assumed that Keary was independent, especially since she'd seen him only once or twice in the New York office before that night in the limo. But now she wondered if Keary did whatever his father wanted. If Jack pressured Keary to get rid of her, would he? Despite the pleasant smile and kind eyes, Jack was a powerful businessman.

"Yes," she whispered. "The baby."

"I want you to come to New York to talk about it," he said.

She didn't think she had a choice, but voiced her feelings anyway. "I don't really fly because the morning sickness never left after the first trimester. It's just dizziness and feeling ill hours afterward that I can't handle."

"Keary has made the preparations already," he continued as if she hadn't spoken. "He will escort you, and we can talk on Wednesday."

"Wednesday? Jack, I—"

"It's settled then. Have a good day, Zacari." He hung up.

Zacari fumed. Did he think he had her in the palm of his hand because he could fire her any time he wanted? Well she wasn't the one. Just like she found this job, she could find the next, and besides, she'd kept up her studies. In a few months, she would have her Bachelors degree and be much more marketable.

She had a few minutes to sit there and rethink the whole flying off the handle for one conversation. Jack hadn't been mean. He wasn't rude. She was a subordinate in his company, and just because her relationship with him had just gotten a lot more personal, didn't mean he would automatically not behave like he would with her in the office, and that was tell her what to do. They would both have some adjustments to make.

Zacari drew in a deep breath, gave Jack the benefit of the doubt, and blew it out. "Woosa," she whispered.

"What's that all about?" one of her coworkers asked as she strolled by.

Zacari wrinkled her nose. "Hey, it's Monday. I have an excuse."

The woman chuckled. "I hear you, girl. Later, hope it's all uphill from here."

"Thanks," Zacari called. "I think."

The phone rang again. Zacari picked it up without looking at the display. "Are you free now?" She jumped at Debbie's voice and snapped up a pen and a note pad. Zacari did not support Debbie at all, but it didn't hurt to be prepared.

"Yes, thanks for being so patient. What can I do for you, Debbie?" The pleasant tone she used grated on her own nerves. She knew it had to piss off Debbie, which wasn't a bad thing. Zacari pressed her lips together to keep from laughing.

"Come into my office, please." The phone went dead.

Zacari went in and didn't wait to be asked to sit down.

She slid into a seat opposite Debbie's desk and waited. Debbie pretended not to notice as she read over a paper in front of her and then signed the bottom. She shuffled a few more items on her desk, and finally stood up to close the door. By the time she sat down again, Zacari was gritting her teeth with impatience. Something told her either Debbie knew about the baby or that she'd had dealings with Keary in the past, and she didn't like it.

At last, Debbie steepled her hands on her desk and leaned forward. Angry blue eyes bore into Zacari's making her shift around on her chair. No, not blue—one blue, one green. So Debbie wore colored contact lenses. Zacari would never have suspected her of it. What else was fake on the woman? Against her will her gaze slid down to Debbie's D size perky breasts.

The woman's eyebrows shot low like Zacari had accused her of something. "I wanted us to be honest with one another from the start," she began. "Keary told me about the baby."

Zacari gasped. "*Keary* told you?"

"Well, he told me that he thought we should wait awhile before we take our relationship to the next level while he took care of some personal business." Her expression hardened. "A friend told me he spotted Keary coming from your apartment a couple days ago. Add to that, how you ran and hid like a scared rabbit when he came to the office, and he couldn't stop looking at you when everyone was welcoming him home that first day. I put two and two together."

Dang, was nothing secret in this office? She scanned her memory to try to remember if any people from the office lived near her. She thought there was this one dude from shipping that she didn't know but recognized. Still, it seemed unlikely that Debbie would even know the man. Then again, stranger things had happened. So she had a spy. That was just great. And she guessed everybody knew by now how much Debbie wanted Keary.

Zacari straightened her back. "My personal life has nothing to do with this office. If you need me to help out on a project and I'm free, I'm sure Jeb will be willing to listen. What you have or *don't have* with Keary is not my concern either. I'm doing my job." Zacari struggled to her feet, annoyed that her clumsy movements didn't punctuate her words like she wanted them to. "If that's all…"

"That's not all!" Debbie surged to her feet, flinging her chair back. Zacari'd always known the woman had anger issues. In her emails to assistants here, more than one had complained about it. That's why Zacari was glad she supported Jeb alone. He was the closest thing to Jack's good nature—well his temperament up until now. The attitude Jack took when they met in person remained to be seen.

Debbie jabbed a finger in Zacari's direction. "I don't know what kind of game you think you're playing, pretending your baby is Keary's, but I'm not dumb enough to fall for it. Keary's not either. He's going along with it now, but he already has plans to get a paternity test."

Zacari's eyes widened. "Excuse me?"

"You heard me, a paternity test. And when he finds out you're nothing but a whore who probably doesn't know who her baby's father is, you'll see all of Keary's money go bye-bye." She waved like a child, but looked stupid doing it.

Zacari's own temper hit the roof at that point. "Look here, I don't know who you think you are, but I'm not the one to be talking to like that. As I said earlier who my baby's father is, is none of your business." She put her hand on the doorknob but turned back to Debbie. "Even at the risk of losing my job, I won't do a damn thing for you. This conversation is over. Don't say anything to me. Don't even look in my direction as you walk by my desk. We're done."

She yanked the door open and let it bang the wall. All eyes in the outside area turned toward them, but Zacari held her head high and waddled to her desk. Not having had time that morning to unpack properly, she just powered down her computer, scooped up her purse and bag, and marched toward the elevators.

"Tell Jeb I'm leaving for the day if he calls in," she yelled to no one in particular and left.

When Zacari got home, she paused at the entrance into the apartment complex and peered around the parking lot. No one was out at this time of day, but she still felt like eyes were on her. She hurried inside and shut the door. After removing her cell phone from her purse, she saw that Keary had called several times, and there were voicemail messages waiting. She rolled her eyes.

The apartment phone rang, but she ignored it. Whatever they all wanted, they could wait until she felt like talking. She stripped and stepped into the shower, being careful to hold onto the rail on the wall. More than once, she'd almost slipped and fallen. It was high time she replaced those lilac flower shaped appliqués that had peeled up a few months ago.

"Not risking you," she whispered to her little one, "even if Keary is planning to ask for a paternity test because he doesn't believe me."

She choked on the last of her words, and the tears she'd fought hard to hold back came streaming down her cheeks. Zacari knew she shouldn't believe anything Debbie said, but she couldn't help feeling hurt at just the thought. And hell, she couldn't blame the man. He didn't know her from Eve. She cried harder. They didn't have a relationship before this all happened. It wasn't like they'd been going out, getting to know each other, and then *bam* a baby.

With her mind going ninety miles a minute, Zacari stepped from the shower, dried off, and headed into her bedroom to put lotion on. The phone rang, and this time she picked it up and then slammed it down. She prayed it wasn't Jeb calling to see if she was okay. If so, she'd explain it tomorrow. By now everyone in the office already knew how whacked out her emotions were half the time. There was no excuse for them, but well, they *knew*.

For most of the day, Zacari found things to do with herself like cleaning up, watching soaps and eating ice cream, and doing laundry. After a small salad at dinner time, she turned off all the lights, plugged her ears with ear buds to listen to music, and drifted off to sleep. At least the phone was silent, and she could think about facing the world tomorrow.

* * * *

At three in the morning, Zacari's eyes popped open. She groaned at the stitch in her side. Her music had stopped, the iPod probably crushed under her big behind. She didn't feel like finding it right now. The steady red light on her bedside phone caught her attention. Messages waited. She reached over for the phone and decided to check them.

To her surprise none were from Jeb, but Keary had left five. The last said, "Zacari, I'm stuck in a meeting, but if you don't call me by five, I will be banging on your door. I'm worried. Call me, damn it!" And he hung up.

She laughed. Sweet, but he hadn't come by. Had he? Or maybe someone told him about the blowup at work. Debbie could have told him lies about what Zacari said and did. She rolled her eyes. Playing these games was not her. While she pondered Keary's thoughts, a powerful craving hit her. All of a sudden, she wanted a tuna melt with a side of coleslaw. She knew just where to get them, but the ride was a bit of a ways from her apartment.

With the phone still in her hand, she bit her lip. Should she call Keary? He acted all like he would be there no matter what, and he didn't want to wait until the baby was born. Cravings were a part of it. She dialed his cell. He picked up on the second ring, although his voice was thick with sleep.

"Zacari? What's wrong? Why didn't you call me? Is the baby okay?"

"Man, let me get a word in edgewise." She chuckled low so he couldn't hear. "I want tuna melts with coleslaw."

"Huh?"

She explained, expecting him to tell her to wait until the morning.

"Surely there's no store open this time of night."

She flopped back on her pillows. The craving

intensified. Her stomach growled since she'd eaten little at dinner. "There is a place I know of. If you're not willing to go, that's all right. I know how to get there. Don't worry about it."

"You will not," he stated emphatically. "Tell me the address, and I'll go."

Her eyes widened. "Right now?"

"Yes, right now."

She couldn't hold back the smile on her face, and her heart did that pitter pat it had done when he rubbed her feet. Zacari knew she was being selfish, and she certainly didn't want to take advantage of him. She'd traveled plenty of times in the middle of the night for whatever food craving hit her. They just hit with a lot more force now that she was pregnant.

After telling him how to get to her favorite restaurant, she hung up. Struggling to her feet, she tucked her arms into the robe she'd tossed at the bottom of the bed. There was no way she'd let Keary see her in the oversized nightie that extended down past her knees. The thing was clean but well-worn.

When she'd started out to the living room, she stopped. Even with the robe on, the nightie hung past its hem and made her look homely. Sighing at her protruding belly, she returned to her room and rummaged for something sexier. Since that didn't exist, at least not in her wardrobe, she just left the nightie off and retied her robe above her belly. The short length stretching to mid-thigh and the silken lilac material was at least cute if not exactly sexy. It would do.

Half hour later when Zacari thought she might kill Keary the first chance she got, he knocked on the door.

She fought her way off the couch, put a fist in her back because it hurt so much, and went to answer.

Her eyes widened at the sight of him. Hair tussled like he hadn't bothered to comb it, pajama bottoms peaking beneath a trench coat, and sneakers with no socks. "Wow," she teased. "I've never seen you look so sexy."

He held up the bag and strolled past her. Zacari was thrown for a loop when he dropped a kiss on her lips. Sensual pleasure snaked through her system, but Keary kept moving as if it was the most natural thing in the world.

He headed toward the kitchen, and she followed dumbfounded. A black bag sat on one of the chairs where he'd left it, and he busied himself unpacking her late night snack. "I should warn you," he announced when she took a seat, "I'm not in the best of moods at this time of night. For that matter, the morning either. Not until I've had my coffee."

"I'll make you some," she offered and was about to rise.

"Sit still." The command was almost a bark, but he followed it with an apologetic look. "See? Don't worry about it. I'll make it later."

Later? Just how long did he plan on staying, she wondered.

Keary slid her food over to her along with a bottle of fruit juice. She thanked him and tucked into it. After the last bite and she had drained the bottle, she leaned back moaning. "Mm, that was exactly what I needed. Thank you so much."

She winced.

He flew on alert making her suppress a laugh. "What's wrong?"

"It's just my back. Seems like around now, like clockwork, my son sits in this spot that tears my back up. Ugh, it drives me nuts." She rubbed at her back, but it did no good.

Keary frowned. "*Our* son. That reminds me. I have something to try on you. Now that you're done eating, I can. Let's go to the living room, and I'll test it out."

"I'm not your guinea pig."

He smirked but held out his hand to help her stand. Zacari was curious so she gave in. If he tried anything funny, she could always smack him. Somehow she didn't think Keary meant her harm. The man seemed genuinely crazy about the baby. With him here all attentive, it made it hard for her to think Debbie had told her the truth. Then again, the question of paternity had to be on his mind. She should bring up the subject, but she was hesitant. Not being alone was nice, and she didn't want to ruin it. Of course they did have to talk about that kiss. He was not her man, and whether he was going to date Debbie wasn't clear.

Keary brought the black bag to the living room. While she watched sitting on the couch, he unzipped it and pulled out a can of tennis balls. Her eyebrows shifted higher. "Seriously? I know you don't expect me to play tennis at this time of night—or this month."

"Trust me."

He opened the container and removed one of the balls. When he told her to turn around with her back to him, she did. From the first roll of the ball over her back, Zacari was in heaven. Knots and pain eased. She felt the tension melt from her muscles. Her limbs went slack along with her jaw. Chin on her chest, she closed her eyes and just enjoyed it.

"Good?" he whispered over her shoulder.

"Mm," she moaned. "Damn, I might come right here." The ball pressed too hard, and she yelped. "Are you crazy? What was that for?"

He grumbled. "You can't say things like that...and moan."

Zacari blinked up at him. "Again, are you crazy? I didn't just get you excited. I mean look at me. I'm not exactly the next cover model. Not that I ever was, but I'm not about to be a plus sized one either."

She lamented over her huge saggy breasts, her wide hips, and the myriad of other flaws on her body. Never having considered herself beautiful, she did think she had some good qualities—before getting pregnant. Now, she had to keep a bra on twenty-four hours a day except when she showered to keep her boobs from sagging permanently. Aside from that, they leaked milk, so she had to keep pads in the cups as well.

"You're kidding," Keary told her. "Zacari, you are still very beautiful, and just the thought of seeing you like *that* without your clothes on gets me worked up."

She looked down at herself when she realized his gaze had locked on her deep cleavage. His pants tented with his erection, so there was no denying Keary was excited. Zacari wanted to put it down to men getting hard-ons for no reason, but she couldn't mistake the desire in his eyes. "You're remembering that night," she assured him. "It was hot and so good. I admit that. Trust me when I tell you it wouldn't be the same this time."

Zacari tried turning her head away from him, but he caught her chin and made her look at him. He leaned in and brushed her lips with the most feathery of touches. A shiver coursed over her skin. She pulled from his grasp, but Keary wouldn't be put off. He dropped the ball and wrapped his arms around her. "Zacari, you cannot be so blind, can you?" At her look which must have reflected her confusion, he grunted. She almost laughed. Okay, Keary wasn't his usual pleasant self, but he wasn't a bear either. The man didn't have real issues like the rest of them. He might be a robot.

She shrugged in response to him. He took on a more serious attitude and began to instruct her.

Chapter Six

"You're breasts are bigger. I saw that right off. No, don't pull away. Woman, most men love breasts. Some think the bigger the better." His eyes almost glazed at the topic of conversation. "For myself, I've always loved them no matter the size, and I have to admit from the moment I saw you, I couldn't help wondering about your nipples."

She gasped. "My nipples?"

"They're bigger too?"

She put her hands up over her peaks like he could see them through her bra and robe. "Maybe. I know they're achy."

"I could soothe them if you let me suck them," he offered.

She squeezed her thighs together. "Now, who's provoking people with their dirty talk?"

He chuckled then licked the tip of her ear. "I want to do a lot more than talk." He ran his hand up her thigh, parting her robe and squeezing her flesh. Yesterday, she'd been lamenting over having thunder thighs.

Keary's stroke brought no such thoughts to mind. Close to spreading her legs, she dropped her hand over his.

"Talk is exactly what we need to do." She pushed him off. "Keary, I won't be the other woman. I'm not helping you cheat on Debbie. And there's some...other stuff we need to discuss."

She twisted around so she could face him and look him in the eyes. To her surprise, the lust hadn't lessened in the least. He didn't even appear to be upset about her mentioning Debbie. "I can't cheat if I'm not seeing her. Stop fighting me. I want to make love to you. Talk can wait until after we've satisfied ourselves."

He took her hand and placed it on his cock. Zacari's mouth went dry when his shaft twitched beneath her touch. She licked her lips. All the willpower in the world didn't stop her from squeezing it and stroking until she almost cried out in need. Before she could pull away, Keary tightened his hold and made her rub harder. He held her gaze, his eyes darkening. His breathing became ragged to match hers. Damn it, she wanted this like nobody's business. She didn't want to think rationally. Hell, it wasn't like there'd be consequences again. She was still pregnant.

When she strained forward and their tongues met, Zacari moaned against Keary's mouth. He tasted her lips for barely a second before he lowered his head to her neck then lower until he reached her cleavage. The man really did have an obsession. But she wasn't ready to let him see her naked or to give in to what they both wanted.

"I'm not sure," she whispered. "I mean how do I know..."

"How does anyone know?" he countered. "Do you

want me to take you to her and have her confirm we're not dating?"

"Not on your life. That would be humiliating—for both her and me." She chewed her bottom lip. "I want to do the right thing. There's so much more going on here. Jack—"

"Forget my father for the moment." He unbelted her robe, sliding each side of the belt from the knot slowly. Zacari's breath caught in her throat. She shivered, thinking to stop him, but her fingers curled instead around the sides of her robe and pushed it wider. She stood up and watched Keary's eyes trace every move she made.

His hunger was palpable. "Will you seduce me again?"

She hesitated. "No, I can't. I shouldn't."

He stood and pushed her robe over her shoulders then drew her close. Embarrassed about the unsexiness of her bra, she didn't say a word. But Keary didn't appear to be put off. He kissed the tender skin on her shoulder, made his way to her chest, and then let his tongue glide across one breast.

"Let me taste your nipple."

Zacari shuddered. "Keary, you don't understand."

He paused to lead her to the bedroom. She was as stiff as a virgin. At the same time, her pussy creamed for him, she couldn't bring herself to believe he'd want her when she was naked. Keary wouldn't take no for an answer. Not that she'd voiced the word. If there was even the slightest chance he'd want to continue, she ached to know it. She might have accused him of remembering that one perfect night, but then so was she. Oh man, how she had ridden him. Would her stamina even last to do it again? She had to know.

Her bra hit the floor. She hadn't been wearing any panties, so now she was naked in front of him. Zacari covered her breasts staring at the floor. Keary dragged her hands down to her sides, but he didn't say a word. She closed her eyes and felt her breath coming in heavy bursts, knew that it made her chest rise and fall too sharply. Embarrassment at her body was so strong, she wanted to disappear. Worse, she felt liquid forming at one of her nipples.

"I've always wondered," Keary said, and she had an instant to think about what he meant. His full lips curved around her nipple, and she cried out in ecstasy when she felt his tongue scoop up the tiny drop. "Oh hell," he murmured.

Keary cupped her heavy breasts in his palms and lifted them to his hungry mouth, first one and then the other. He alternated between licking and nuzzling each nipple. Zacari sagged forward, catching herself on his shoulder. The sensations he sent through her body made her weak. She would have dropped to the floor, if Keary didn't pull her carefully into his arms and carry her to the bed. She could have come just feeling the strength in his arms, seeing the intensity in his gaze.

"I'm amazed," he said, leaning over her and circling an areola with his fingertip. "The taste is different from last time, yet good. I can't believe how it turns me on all the more knowing I have to be careful not to hurt you. I didn't, did I?"

"No. What you did was make me hotter. So, I don't turn you off?"

For the second time, he led her hand to his cock. His

piece was longer than she remembered and thicker. Of course it was probably the same, and the fact that Zacari hadn't had sex in six months made her more desperate. Keary made her rub, heightening her need, and it seemed to drive him crazy.

She loved watching his head dip back and his eyes close. His massive chest rose and fell, reminding her of how his skin tasted. Had he dreamed of their time together as she had done over the last few months? "Can I taste you?" she almost begged.

He practically ripped his T-shirt over his head. "Not my cock, but anywhere else." The pajama bottoms settled beside his shirt on the floor. Zacari lusted over his bare chest. She wasted no time exploring, pinching his nipples, and following her fingers with her mouth. Zacari teased him with the tip of her tongue. She loved his salty flavor. Inching closer, she ran her palms over his rippled abs. *Oh yes, I remember this body.* Her pussy clenched as the memories washed over her, of their movements, their moans, the sounds of their bodies slapping together as Keary had taken her hard and fast.

This time it had to be gentler, and she wondered if it would be good despite that. Keary seemed to read her mind. He coaxed her to her back and positioned himself between her legs. Tracing her lips with his thumb, he stared down at her. "Don't worry. I'm going to make you come over and over, baby. Do you want that?"

Zacari couldn't answer because he reached between her legs and caught her clit. He pinched lightly causing her to clench her jaw. So soon, she was about to rocket to climax. She held on a little longer.

"Yes," she huffed. "I want that. I want it so much."

He pushed a single finger into her pussy. Her cream coated his digit. "And this?" he asked. "Do you want this?"

"Yes, oh yes, Keary!"

He added another finger and then another. Stroking in and out of her, he took his time, teasing her, making her ache to come. His movements quickened, and Zacari bunched her hands in the sheets. When she was close to orgasm, he slowed his pace. She whimpered and shook. Keary leaned down to kiss her while keeping up his tormenting rhythm. Zacari couldn't concentrate. She let him take her bottom lip between his and cried out when he nipped it. He knew just how to make her crazy. In one night, he learned her quirks, the various pleasure spots that would take her to the brink.

To prove he knew just what to do, Keary pulled out his fingers and switched to using his thumb. The pad rotated over her clit in measured circles. Zacari squeezed her thighs together, trapping his hand.

"Uh-uh, baby," he warned, pulling her legs apart and holding one still, "let me make you come."

Zacari thrashed on the bed. Her inner muscles coiled tight in readiness for her release. She rode his hand, holding him to her and wiggling her hips. Just when she thought she would scream if she didn't come right now, Keary took it to another level. He used one hand to play with her throbbing clit and the other he moistened in her juices before circling her anus. When he put pressure at back entrance, she screamed and came hard. Shuddering, she called out his name as wave after wave rolled over her being.

Even after the explosion, Keary seemed to know her

body. He teased her little clit until a second tiny orgasm tumbled through her and then a third. Afterward, gasping for breath, she lay still and watched him through slits. "You remember it all," she whispered.

"I do."

She wanted to ask why but didn't. Rather she enjoyed the fact that a man like him who could have any woman he wanted hadn't forgotten her.

But Keary hadn't reached his release. He hesitated and leaned back staring at her pussy like it called to him. She knew how he liked the taste of come and was surprised and a little disappointed that he didn't eat her out. Her cream flowed. Even making herself come over the last few months hadn't produced so much. No one had made her as wet as Keary did.

"So wet," he commented, but didn't move to take her. "Are you tired?"

Now she realized what he was doing. He worried about wearing her out. The man had no idea. Already, her pussy anticipated being filled with his big cock. In fact just looking at it, she imagined taking it into her mouth and draining him. Her body was still on fire. She might not be able to take him all night, but her desire was sky high.

"You wouldn't deny me, would you, Daddy?" She pouted, something she never did, but the situation seemed to call for it. The words paired with a soft sexy voice, she watched his reaction.

Keary's shaft twitched. He scooted closer, pulled her thighs so she eased into position, and he pushed the head of his cock against her opening. "Just a little bit, baby. I need to get inside you for just a while."

His cock pushed past her folds. Zacari began to shake, and Keary sucked in a noisy breath. He grunted as he pressed in. His cock was so thick, she felt him forcing her wider. She held as still as she could so he wouldn't think he was hurting her and stop. The sensations were far from pain. Bliss suffused her. Against her will, her inner muscles clenched, almost sucking Keary in to stroke his long, wide erection.

Zacari couldn't help herself. She began moving her hips, coaxing him deeper. He tried taking his time, but twice his thrusts sped up. She watched him grit his teeth biting down and fighting for control. Zacari wanted him to lose it, to pound her until she cried. Her lust was out of control, but she was glad Keary was stronger.

He stroked the full length of his cock from base to tip along the sides of her pussy. She arched her hips and helped him to drive in. When their hips drew apart, it was like they'd been separated for years. Zacari pushed forward at the same time that Keary did. Their bodies came together in a quiet slap.

He belongs right there, deep inside of me. Let him take me forever. It's so good, Keary. Silly of her to fall for him, but she was already addicted.

Keary lifted her thighs and squeezed the backs of her knees. He dragged her tighter to his cock and shoved all the way in. When he paused she got to know just how full she was with all of him in her. He shuddered, leaning over her, eyes closed and seeming to struggle.

"Don't hold it, baby." She ran her fingers along his thigh, reveling in the hard muscle. "Come on, Daddy, fill me up."

That did it. Keary thrust fast but not hard. He threw

his head back and shouted. His hot seed shot into her pussy. Zacari wiggled her hips, and Keary fell to the side. He caught himself on the bed with one arm while he made sure his cock didn't come out. For a few more moments, he thrust into her, and then finally let himself collapse on the bed.

She thought he was done, but Keary knew her from their night together. He rolled to his side and cupped her pussy with one hand. Their mouths tangled together in hungry kisses while he worked her into her fourth orgasm.

Ready to purr like a well-sexed kitten, Zacari tried to get up and just now remembered her belly. Keary was such an amazing lover, he made her forget how her body looked. The lust in his eyes, the caresses of his hands made her feel sexy.

He reached out a hand to support her elbow as she rose.

"Thanks," she murmured, eyelids lowered. Together they went into the bathroom, and he sat her on the commode while he readied the shower. Zacari's heart did flip-flops as she watched him. What if this was permanent? What if he was always here no matter the time of day or night to care for her? She shook her head to jiggle the thoughts from her mind. No use working herself up over Keary. Too often she remembered her ex-boyfriend and what he'd done, how he cheated right under her nose. If she let Keary into her heart, he might do the same. Sure, all men weren't alike, and Keary might not mean it, but their relationship, if one could call this budding interaction a relationship, was an accident. Already she loved her son, and she believed Keary did too, but that didn't change the fact that neither of them would have chosen to bring him into the world this way.

Keary frowned at the bottom of the shower. "There's nothing to make it less slippery, and you shower in here?"

She shrugged. "No choice, don't wanna stink."

"Not acceptable. I'll get some later today. I'm glad I'm here to help you now. Come on, I'll wash you."

Her eyes widened. "Y-You don't have to do that for me. I won't fall." She avoided telling him about the near misses.

"Of course I do. You are carrying my baby." His words were kind, but they hurt just the same. Zacari wouldn't have changed what he said though. That Keary was doing all this because she was having his child was something she needed to remember. He didn't love her and never would.

When she stood up, he covered her lips with his and kissed her until she was ready for another round of sex. Keary angled her face toward him and pushed his tongue deeper into her mouth. All thoughts of their situation fluttered away under his sensual onslaught. Zacari closed her mouth around Keary's tongue while he pumped in and out. The act made her think of what he's just finished doing with her pussy. She squirmed.

After a few moments, he pulled back and led her into the shower. The water was warm enough to chase away the descending chill when she stepped into bathroom. Keary positioned himself behind her so that she took most of the spray. His hands flattened over her sides, and he kissed her shoulder. "Hand me the body wash."

Tingling in anticipation, Zacari gave him the tea tree and lavender scented shower gel. He squeezed off some into his hand and dipped it in the water before working up a lather. Zacari should have known he'd go right for her breasts. And she should have known his fingertips moving over her nipples, slippery with suds, would have her peaks pebbling in no time.

She groaned and arched into his touch. Keary played with her breasts, weighing their heaviness in his palms and then moved over her swelling belly. When his hand dipped between her legs, she braced herself on the support bar and spread her legs.

"I know you want to come again," he whispered in her ear.

"Keary," she breathed, "stop teasing."

"Why should I? Tell me you don't want it."

She wouldn't say that. She wanted to beg for it. He didn't wait for her consent but rubbed along her slit without piercing it. Zacari whined with each stroke. She wanted him to delve deeper so bad but held on.

"Do you trust me, Zacari?"

She gasped at his question, and her eyes which had drifted closed popped open. Trust? What was he getting at? "What do you mean?"

He dropped a gentle kiss on her shoulder. "I mean if I give you a couple of instructions, will you obey me and not question what I'm doing?"

A question already trembled on her lips, but the excitement of not knowing what was to come kept her quiet. When she didn't respond, he moved his fingers away from her pussy. Zacari could have wept. Keary reached past her and angled the shower head away from them. When he began lowering them both to the tub, she squeaked but didn't protest.

Keary ended up beneath her while she sat on his lap. Her body had become so bulky over the last month or so, she'd found it easier to just shower rather than risk getting stuck in the tub. Keary had no such problem, but he hadn't plugged the drain, so she had no idea where he was going with this.

"Lean into me," he instructed.

She did, and he slung a heavy arm over the top of her chest to keep her in place. With his other hand, he reached down between her legs. All of a sudden, Zacari knew, and her need skyrocketed. Keary pushed two fingers into her pussy without ceremony. Zacari barely got to enjoy the entry before he pulled back out and used her thick cream to coat her anus. Goose bumps riddled her skin.

"Keary…"

"Trust me."

When her back entrance was coated and slick, Keary began working a single digit into her hole. Zacari's breath left her body in a whoosh. She whimpered at the intense pleasure, the very slight ache of his breach. Keary added another finger to stretch her wider. She chewed her bottom lip, closed her eyes, and buried her face into his neck.

"Does it hurt too much?" he asked.

"Uh-uhn." She didn't look up. Waves of ecstasy rocked her, but she held on.

"Do you want me to stop?"

"You better not," she almost shouted.

He chuckled. Another finger went in. Keary pumped three fingers in and out of her ass, slapping the heel of his hand against her pussy with each entrance. Zacari bucked a little and wriggled on his lap. His cock, solid and unyielding under her twitched to join the action, but Keary concentrated on pleasuring her first with his hands.

Hungry for him, Zacari found his mouth and snaked her tongue inside. Their lips locked together, sucking and exploring each other's warm depths. Now she knew why he hadn't eaten her. Keary wanted to kiss her more. Just the act seemed to make him harder, and he didn't want her to taste her own juices right now.

He broke the kiss but left his lips brushing hers. "Do you want me to fuck you up your ass?"

She gasped at the harsh, dirty words. He'd not done that before, but it turned her on big time. "Yes, Daddy, fuck me, please."

Keary's eyes burned with his lust. He pulled his fingers from her anus and then hoisted her hips higher. With her resting on his abs, he guided his cock to her tight hole. Zacari breathed deeply to keep herself relaxed. From the wide head's first piercing, her pussy pulsed, and her core muscles clenched.

Zacari tried leaning up, but Keary pulled her back and lifted her knees higher. "No, baby, you must stay at this angle so I don't hurt you."

He pushed in farther. She groaned. He pinned her down while he filled her to capacity. Zacari couldn't do a thing other than enjoy his slow movements in and out of her. When his cock was deep inside, he grasped her hips and raised her up and down his length. She cried out his name, and Keary matched it by grunting hers.

"Damn, you're so tight, baby. Your body feels so good, I'm going to come."

Keary worked her faster. Zacari's muscles squeezed him tighter, sucking him in. With each thrust her swollen breasts bounced, so she held them in place. Her hands grazed the sensitive nipples, making her hotter. She threw her head back and coaxed Keary to pump harder. Their bodies moved in perfect unison while the shower spray rained down on them and cooled their heated skin.

"Fuck, yes," Keary roared. His seed spilled inside of her, and he spasmed, pinching her hips to grind her into him. She screamed his name as an orgasm took hold. Although Keary had reached his release, he didn't stop pumping until she'd ridden hers to completion.

At last they lay quiet in each other's arms, Keary resting his cheek against her forehead. She struggled to regain control of her breathing while he stroked her belly. *Stupid, stupid me. I love him.*

After a while, Keary stood them both on their feet with no problems, impressing Zacari with his strength. He washed her from head to toe and then himself. When he'd dried them both, he lifted Zacari into his arms and carried her to the bed. "Sleep, beautiful. I will come back later, and we'll talk. Agreed?"

She yawned and nodded. At peace and utterly satisfied, Zacari drifted off to dreamland. Although Keary had left her apartment to return to his, the memory of his touch stayed with her the rest of the night and into most of the morning.

Chapter Seven

Keary woke with one thing on his mind, or rather one woman—Zacari. Having her again had been explosive, just like it had been the first time. Her breasts so big and full made him harder than he thought possible. At first, he'd thought he was some kind of pervert for being ready to come seeing her naked with her swollen belly, especially when he got off on sucking the milk from her nipples. Just remembering hardened his cock. He put a hand behind his head and sighed.

Then of course he recalled that this was a sexy beautiful woman, and no matter what condition she was in, he wanted her. He ached to be inside of her, to fill her until she screamed his name. And Zacari had shouted it all right. He grinned. Jack had raised him to know his mind, to set his sights on what he wanted, and then to go after it.

While he did know his mind, for the life of him, he couldn't figure out what Zacari had on him aside from the baby. What drew him to her was a mystery, and just how deep those feelings went. Well now wasn't the time to think on it. He had to get a couple hours in at work, and then he would pick up Zacari to talk about their situation.

He'd known by the irritation in her voice last night when she suggested that he go get her snack that she was angry about the call to New York. And when she mentioned Jack, he had no doubts that his father had treated her like an employee rather than as the mother of his grandson. Keary felt the dopey grin spread over his face when he thought of his son. "*My* son."

That's why he couldn't figure things out, he decided. Because he already loved his son, and Zacari was the woman who was delivering such a valuable gift to him. Right now, he couldn't separate thoughts of his son from her. Aside from the sex of course.

He swung his feet over the side of his bed just as the cell phone on the nightstand buzzed. Keary glanced at it and saw that it was Debbie. He frowned. He'd been clear to her that he needed some time. Not that he had totally given up on her. The fact remained that they were a good match in likes and dislikes, and that they had much in common. He could talk to her about business or current events for hours on end. And hell, she was drop-dead gorgeous. But right now, he needed to focus on Zacari.

The fact that he was even thinking of Debbie this way annoyed him as well, especially because when he got around Zacari, all he could think about was her. These feelings, this confusion was unlike him. He'd never felt seriously about a woman and wanted another. And he definitely couldn't sleep with one while meeting the mind of the other. Maybe if he got to know Zacari, they could connect on an intellectual level, or if the baby hadn't surprised them, he could have been intimate with

Debbie, and what he'd started with her would have been cemented.

Growling in frustration, he answered the phone. "Hello."

"Oh." Debbie's tone was hesitant. "I'm sorry to bother you, Keary."

Instantly, he was contrite. He hadn't meant to sound like a bear. Last night, he'd warned Zacari he could be a grump before his coffee, but he'd proceeded to enjoy his time with her. *Zacari again.* He sighed and shook her from his thoughts. "I apologize, Debbie. I didn't get sleep much last night. What can I do for you?"

She didn't speak right away, and he was about to prod her again. Keary assumed she would launch into a conversation about their stuttered relationship, but she was all business. "It's about the Shore Project. Jack wants me to fly up tomorrow and spend the rest of the week with him and Jeb going over the figures. He says we'll be at his house so there'll be fewer distractions. You already know how big this thing could get, so he's not taking any chances."

Keary's eyes widened. His father's house! Jack knew he'd invited Zacari to his house so they could discuss the baby and for him to get to know Zacari on a personal level. There wasn't a doubt in his mind that Jack hadn't forgotten. He considered if this was a plot on his father's part to sabotage whatever he thought was going on between Keary and Zacari. After all Keary hadn't made it a secret that he was talking to Debbie while in Cairo. Then again, Jack was not the type to pull tricks like this. He dealt above the table at all time, whether it was in business or his personal life. If Jack didn't like something, he made it known. Keary had to believe this was all about the project. This opportunity could mean millions. Jack wouldn't risk losing it because the key personnel were in another state. And the man could multi-task better than anyone Keary knew.

"Yes, I'm aware," he finally admitted. "However, I'm not on that project." He hesitated about admitting he'd be in New York.

"Oh, I know. It's just that I need your help. I don't want to go to Jack unprepared. I need to use all of my resources to get the figures he needs, so I'm using mine—you."

He narrowed his eyes, saying nothing and hoping she wasn't just coming up with an excuse to get close to him again. It had been Debbie who made it clear she was interested when they first began talking. Keary had followed up right away because he had been as well.

"Keary, are you there?" she called down the line.

"I'm here."

She seemed to grow desperate and then calmed herself. "You have a rapport with Eve over at Lancing Associates. I need to get her input fast, and she's been putting me off for weeks. I have a meeting with her this afternoon. Please, Keary," she coaxed. "I have to go to New York tomorrow to meet with Jack. I don't want to go without the information from Eve. Will you go with me? I will make it worth your while."

Keary sighed, rubbing the back of his neck. He'd needed to talk to Zacari this afternoon, and something told him if he put off talking, she'd be pissed. She'd think he didn't want to talk since he'd been consumed with thoughts of sex when they were together. Still, he understood Debbie's plight. Eve was notorious for being stubborn. And hell she could be. She was a brilliant businesswoman and held a key component for their project. Debbie attending Jack's meeting without her input was tantamount to getting her walking papers.

"All right, I'll go. What time is the meeting?" Maybe he could see Zacari before it.

"Four. Thank you. I promise, I will make it up to you." Her tone had dropped to sensual, but Keary pretended not to have picked up on it. He glanced at the clock. Damn, he'd slept until two. There was no time to run to Zacari's before the meeting.

"Okay, I'll meet you at her office at three forty-five. Talk to you later." He disconnected the call before she could say more. He had just enough time to shower, prepare some notes, and get over there. He phoned Zacari, but she didn't answer. When her voicemail came on, he left a brief explanation and hung up.

* * * *

Eve let out a high-pitched squeak and hurried on the tips of her toes toward Keary, arms outstretched. "My favorite person in the world. How are you, Keary?" She latched onto his arm and kissed his cheek. "It's been forever. Why don't you come visit your cousin anymore? She pointedly ignored Debbie at his side.

Keary grunted. "We're hardly cousins, Eve. Your 'uncle' married my second cousin, a relationship established solely for business."

She pouted. Eve was not the most attractive woman, he'd always thought, but she made up for it in untouchable self-confidence. Besides that, she was a ruthless businesswoman. For some reason, she loved him and hated his father. Keary could not abide the way she pretended to be the delicate female with men while railroading them out of their companies behind their backs. He'd long suspected she was the brains behind the man she called uncle taking Keary's cousin's company, which was also the reason Jack hated her. He'd been waiting for his chance to bring her down, and Keary thought this project was his father's opportunity.

"Aw, don't be mean, Keary, honey, I've missed you. Can't you say you've missed me?" She tugged him in the direction of her office. "I know you have. You could see me every day if you'd only take my offer of vice president. I'd double what you're getting from that old fart, Jack."

Keary pasted a smile on his face. "Sorry, sweetie. What I do for Jack isn't exactly a job. I own a good portion of the company. Thanks for the offer."

When they were seated in her lavish office with a real wood desk that could be considered a conference table, Debbie made her presence known. "Eve, thanks for seeing me. I wanted to discuss those figures for the—"

"So, Keary, what do you think of the Shore Project?" Eve interrupted. "Do you think it's viable for me?"

Debbie's face reddened. Keary suppressed his irritation. He leaned back and unbuttoned his suit jacket. "I'm sure you've gone over the figures a hundred times and had your accountant review it with you. You're no doubt discussed it with half a dozen of your executives. What you intend to do now will be based on whether you want to continue to thwart Jack's efforts, or use this to your advantage somewhere down the line."

She had been perched on the end of her desk in front of him, obviously hoping he'd enjoy the view of her long legs and spiked heels. Keary hadn't allowed his eyes to go lower than her chin. Eve stood up and stomped around the desk to take her seat. "You're so much like Jack—straightforward. When will you learn a little guile, a little trickery, Keary? Come on, you've got to play the game."

He smiled. "I believe I do okay."

She nodded, eyes narrowed and focused on his face. "Yes, you're your father's son all right. Both of you will smile in a person's face while ripping the shirts off their backs."

"I prefer the direct approach," he countered. "I think it's more upfront than to do it in secret. Besides, all of my father's and my associates come out better than they began with our negotiations. Not many can say the same."

The blood suffusing her cheeks meant Eve knew he referred to her as being underhanded and stripping those she did business with. She wanted games, and they'd played this one before. Keary made it clear he didn't like her methods, but Eve didn't care about that. She wanted to believe despite those feelings, he wanted her because powerful men were often attracted to powerful women. If she only knew the truth—he'd shave his head and become a monk rather than take her to bed. Eve was far from being his type.

At their banter, Debbie laid a hand on his arm, her eyes widening in alarm. He figured Keary was ruining any chance of getting Eve on board. "Hey, take it easy," she whispered. "We want her with us, remember?"

He was not concerned in the least and said aloud. "Don't worry, Debbie, I believe Eve knows a good thing when she sees it, and we can count on her involvement in the Shore Project."

Eve sat in silence sulking. Keary knew her well. She would be stubborn as long as possible, make it look like she wouldn't do it, and even try pushing them into begging her. But eventually, she would give in.

"If you weren't interested," Keary continued, "you would have said no right away. Am I correct?"

When she frowned, he thought he might have pushed her too far, but then her mood—as it often did—shifted. A sunny smile broke out on her face, and she stood up. "I'm hungry. Keary, take me to dinner."

"My pleasure," he said simply. Inside, he growled in frustration. This was further delay in seeing Zacari. He stood up prepared to wine and dine this annoying woman until she gave him what he wanted. He'd keep it professional of course because there was no way in hell he'd sleep with a woman to get her business.

As they prepared to leave, Eve tossed a glance over her shoulder at Debbie and sighed. "I guess you can come too, but when things get hot with me and Keary, you get lost."

Behind Eve's back, Debbie looked like she would launch herself onto her, teeth gritted and fingers curled, long nails ready to rip into Eve. Keary took a step back to allow Eve to pass him out the door and caught Debbie mid-lunge.

He took a firm hold of her arm and kept her at his side. He pitched his voice low and made sure they were a few more paces behind Eve. "Calm down. She does it to provoke you. She knows there will never be anything between us, and she's pissed off that you're so much more beautiful."

At his compliment, Debbie preened and clung to him, pressing a breast into his arm. Zacari's naked form flashed through his mind, her full, sensitive breasts ready for his hands and his mouth. He put space between him and Debbie.

"This isn't the time for that. If you let on about the attraction between us, Eve will not deal. Debbie accepted his explanation, and backed off. Keary led both women into the elevator, and they descended to the parking garage.

When they arrived at the restaurant Eve had chosen, he tried twice to reach Zacari, but she didn't answer. He punched the drop button and tucked the phone into his shirt pocket. For the next couple of hours, they ate, drank, and spoke of anything other than business. By the time, Debbie and Eve had had a few drinks, they were more tolerant of each other. Keary kept his alcohol to nursing one glass of Tom Collins.

Eve leaned forward and rested a hand on his thigh. "Why so quiet, Keary, baby? Aren't you having a good time?"

"Of course. I always have a good time with you." He smiled and took the hand off his leg, but did not kiss it or caress it as she probably wanted him to.

Eve popped up to her feet. "I want to dance. Let's go dancing, Keary." She spun to Debbie almost losing her footing. "I know plenty of sexy men who would do anything for me. I can give you one, and we could dance all night."

Debbie'd had too many martinis. "S-sure, but keep him for yer-s-self. I'll take Keary." Her words slurred so much, he didn't think Eve had understood. Eve wiggled her hips, got her feet tangled and landed on his lap just as his phone rang.

He moved to haul her off of him, when Eve giggled and found the phone in his pocket. He lunged for it, but she was too fast. She rolled onto the floor at the same time pressing the connect button. "Hello," she cooed into the phone. "This is Keary's phone, his lover speaking."

Keary snatched the phone away from her, not caring if he'd been a little too rough. Eve's face reddened, and she whimpered "ouch, that hurt." He ignored her to look down at the phone. The line had gone dead. In checking caller ID, he found what he dreaded most. Zacari had called.

"This night is over," he barked. "Get up, Eve. I'm taking you *both* home."

She struggled to her feet, her face a mask of drunken confusion. He settled the bill and hauled them both by their elbows. As Eve stumbled along, she mumbled, "What about the deal?"

"Take it or leave it," he ground out. "Get the paperwork on Debbie's desk by seven a.m., or we're no longer interested."

She fell into the front seat of his car. "Fine, I'll take it. The papers are already signed. I'll send a carrier."

Keary slammed the door in her face. He'd reached his limit. Most of the time, it took a lot to make him lose his temper, but knowing Eve's games had made Zacari assume he was out having sex with another woman rather than talk to her had taken him there. He remembered everything about that night they met, including the fact that she'd been drinking because her boyfriend had cheated on her with her best friend. While his and Zacari's relationship wasn't defined, they had just been in bed together, and he'd be the lowest man on the planet to leave her bed only to find another woman's the next night.

While he did thirty miles over the speed limit, he dialed her. She didn't answer. He dared not leave a message with the two other women in the car. No telling what other stupid remarks would come out of Eve's mouth. Gripping the steering wheel harder, he ground his teeth. All this on top of the fact that Debbie would be in New York at his father's house.

He considered taking her to his apartment, but she might think he was ashamed of her or thought she wasn't good enough to stay at his father's house. Not being sure of the atmosphere or what was on Jack's mind, he didn't want to put more strain on her than necessary. There was no right solution. He'd just have to do the best he could, and that would start with him talking to her. Slamming his fist on the steering wheel, he pressed harder on the gas. No matter what the time, he would go to her place. He needed to explain and be sure she was okay. Work could damn well wait.

Chapter Eight

Zacari yanked clothes from her closet and more from her dresser. Her room looked like a cyclone hit it. She shouldn't let Keary get to her, but she couldn't help it. She'd cried when she hung up the phone. Stupid of her for falling in love with him and thinking that last night was special. Why would it be? It was sex.

She brushed the wetness from her cheeks and dragged her suitcase to the top of the bed. An ache started in her side, and muscles in her stomach spasmed. She winced, rubbing her belly and breathing deeply until it eased. If she had this baby tomorrow it wouldn't be soon enough.

That thought stopped her in her tracks. "No. Hell no! He's not going to affect the health of my son." She looked down at her belly. "I'm sorry, sweetie. Everything is okay. Stop kicking Mommy now."

She laughed. Her son could sense everything that happened to her, especially when she was upset. Last week she'd treated herself to a movie, an intense one that made her scream out loud at points. Her son had kicked like a field kicker in a football game. She'd learned her lesson with that and would wait until after he was born to see anything that would scare her.

The phone rang and buzzed on the nightstand, but Zacari ignored it. Let the bastard wonder what she was thinking. He'd gotten caught, like they always do. Zacari wasn't an idiot. She knew Keary was smart enough not to let that woman answer the phone. In fact, she thought she heard a growl of anger just before she hung up. Whatever. That didn't change the fact that he'd been with her in the first place. And here he had been trying to convince her he wasn't seeing Debbie. Probably seeing them both.

She stomped through the apartment to the living room and searched through her purse. "Damn it, where is it?" She hadn't been able to leave it to Jack or Keary to know she might need a doctor's note to say she could fly. Some airlines had no restrictions, but others did, and since neither Jack nor Keary had bothered to tell her which one they were taking, she had to be prepared.

A few hours later, Zacari was all packed with her bag still on the bed. She wasn't sure how long they were staying, whether it was one night or several, but she was prepared. Earlier, she'd considered telling them both what cliff to jump off, but she still needed her job. One thing was for sure, when she got back to Chicago, she'd start looking for something else. Maybe no one would want to hire a woman so far along, but she'd never know unless she tried.

Weary and yawning, she checked the clock. Eleven thirty. She should have been in bed ages ago. Her stomach growled. "Of course you're hungry now that it's time to go to bed, she grumbled heading to the kitchen. In the refrigerator, nothing seemed appealing, not even her staple from last week, tacos.

The bell rang followed by a couple pounds on the door. Zacari jumped, her heart thumping in her chest. Who in the hell would be visiting this time of night? And then she remembered Keary. She thought about not answering, but something told her he'd keep knocking and disturb the neighbors.

She found the bat she kept in the corner by her tiny bookshelf and grasped it as she approached the door. "Who is it?"

"It's me. Let me in, Zacari, so we can talk," Keary called out.

"I'll see you in the morning when you pick me up for the airport," she replied. "Oh wait, you never bothered telling me what time did you? All I knew was what day I was being summoned!"

"Baby, don't be that way. Please, let me in. We'll talk."

She had a flashback to Melvin, her ex, when she'd told him she never wanted to set eyes on him. "Aw, baby, don't be that way." Keary might sound sincere, but jerks were the same. They all had the same vocabulary.

"I'm in bed!"

He fell silent, and she thought he'd given up, but he knocked harder and longer. "I can keep this up for hours. Think your neighbors will mind?"

She let out a small screech of anger and unlocked the door. When she'd wrenched it open, she didn't look at him but pivoted to return her bat to the corner. Behind her Keary stepped in and locked the door. She picked up her pace back to her bedroom, hoping he wouldn't touch her because already, flashes of them in each other's arms were zinging across her conscious.

Keary followed her into the bedroom and paused in the doorway. "Wow, looks like a cyclone hit."

Zacari glared at him and headed to her suitcase. "If you're here to tell me how it wasn't you, it wasn't you fault, or the whole thing was a misunderstanding, save it. You're not my man." She put a hand to her lip and said with as much sarcasm as she could inflict into her tone, "Why do I feel like I've said that before?"

"If you'll just…"

She grunted tugging on her suitcase. Keary rushed over to take it from her. "Don't ever lift anything heavy. Ask me, and I'll do it for you."

"Aren't you sweet." She rolled her eyes.

His face fell, and she could have sworn he was hurt before he schooled his features. "Now that I think of it, I'm sure you won't believe me. I remember what you said that night we met, that your boyfriend had cheated on you."

"Ex."

"Your ex. I think you deserve an explanation at least, even if we aren't sure what we are at this point. As of last night, we were at least lovers. I do not jump out of bed with one woman and move on to the next." Zacari remained quiet pretending she wasn't listening to him as she straightened her room. He continued speaking as if she was. "I have a business associate whom Jack would like to come in on a project he's putting together. For whatever reason, she is…uh…attracted to me. I haven't encouraged it. Earlier, I needed to meet with her and Debbie to finalize the agreement. She got smashed and acted less than professional, hence the stupid words on the phone she snatched from my pocket. That's all."

Zacari dropped the blouse in her hand and stared at him. Keary had spoken each word in a robotic monotone. She wasn't ready to believe him of course. Did business people behave that way? *Okay never mind, of course they do. I've seen some of them when they've had a little too much to drink.* Not a pretty sight.

"What time are we leaving tomorrow?" she asked rather than discuss his night out.

Keary walked over to her and lifted her chin, but Zacari pulled away. She went to the bathroom to be sure she hadn't missed any of the toiletries. She wanted them in her bag but accessible in the morning when she got up to get ready. Keary came behind her and lifted the small bag as if that was too heavy for her to handle too. With a noisy breath, she followed him out.

"What you do in your personal life is not my concern. What time are we *leaving*, I asked."

"You're not even going to comment on what I just said?" he grumped. She gave him a look. "I mean more than that. Zacari, I want us to work things out before we go to New York."

"And I don't give a crap." She whipped away from him to mentally go over everything she'd packed and to figure out if she'd forgotten something crucial. Keary sighed and let fall a few words she didn't catch but figured were curses.

He stalked across the room to her doorway and muttered, "six" and then slammed out of the front door. As soon as she knew he was gone, Zacari sunk to the floor and cried. When she remembered she'd have trouble getting up, she cried harder and then laughed at herself for being stupid.

Late that night, she fell into a restless sleep after spending too long thinking about whether Keary was the good man he seemed to be. Before tonight, she thought he'd given her nothing to doubt him over, and his explanation did make sense. When she convinced herself that it didn't matter, that they didn't need to be in a relationship to be good parents, she finally got some sleep. Too soon, though, her alarm clock sounded at five in the morning.

* * * *

Zacari pretended to be asleep for the entire flight to New York so Keary wouldn't bother her. At one point when she could no longer stand the crick in her neck from leaning one way, Keary reached out to gently lay her head on his shoulder. After that, Zacari did fall asleep and didn't rouse until Keary woke her at LaGuardia.

Near the baggage claim, a limo driver held up a sign that read "Keary O'Connor". This time Zacari wasn't so amazed by the luxury which was a part of Keary's everyday life. She let him place a hand at her lower back and guide her into the car. When she was settled, he slipped in beside her, his hard thigh brushing hers. A shock of delight heated her pussy, but Zacari scooted away before the feeling got out of hand. She felt Keary's eyes on her, but she didn't meet his gaze.

Sooner than she expected, they arrived at a beautiful but brick house, nestled among many trees. The house was a good size, but grounds eclipsed it. Keary commented,

"Jack likes intimacy. He likes to keep his family close. Since I have only one sister and my stepmother, this was more than enough. Of course the grounds had to be expansive. He loves to ride as do I."

He thinks this is small?

"You have horses?" she said aloud.

He nodded.

The limo pulled up to the front door. She'd wanted to ask him why he always called his father Jack rather than Dad, which to her didn't sound like the intimacy Jack liked, but he was already opening the door to get out. Zacari followed him. From habit she was going to go to the back of the car to get her suitcase, but Keary blocked her path. Zacari glared at him. Damn, it wasn't like she was some kind of modern woman who hated men doing things for her. She just forgot since she'd been used to handling her own with no one to help.

Rolling her eyes at him, she turned around and walked up the two steps leading to the door. It sat open, and Keary half expected a servant or something, but the small pretty redhead standing there to greet them had to be Keary's stepmother.

"Hello, you must be Zacari," she said with a friendly smile. She pulled Zacari into a hug which shocked her. "I'm so glad to meet you. Come in."

"Mom," Keary said and kissed the woman on the cheek when she moved to him. So this woman he called Mom but didn't extend the same to his father. Zacari looked at Keary and saw genuine affection there. She wondered where his mother was.

Keary introduced the two of them when they were all in the house. Zacari clutched her hands together in front of her. "Nice to meet you, Mrs. O'Connor. You have a beautiful home."

"Sweetie, called me Claudia and thank you."

Claudia showed them to their room. Zacari breathed a sigh of relief when she found that she wouldn't be sharing with Keary. Now that she was inside and on the second floor, the house seemed bigger than it appeared outside. There had to be at least seven bedrooms. This was intimate to Jack.

No one had said where Jack was, or maybe she hadn't been paying attention. All Zacari wanted to do was get this meeting over with and get back home. Even though she was having his grandchild, Zacari hoped to just fall off of Jack's radar and do her own thing. So far, everyone had been nice and all, but these people wouldn't have her in their home if she hadn't gotten freaky with Keary and gotten pregnant. Period. Maybe she was cynical, but it was how she felt.

A knock sounded at her door which she'd closed planning to take a nap before dinner. Zacari walked across to open it. When her gaze met Keary's green one, her heart did flip-flops, and butterflies unsettled her stomach. "Your suitcase," he announced and held it up as proof.

She knew better than to reach for it but rather took a few steps back to let him pass. Just before his bicep brushed across her breasts as he passed, she moved out of reach. As if it had made contact, her body heated up. Tears pricked her eyes. She wanted him to hold her and let her feel his strength and warmth.

Neither of them spoke a word, and when Keary was ready to leave, he stopped in front of her. She stared at the wall just past him. "Listen," he said, and she glanced up at him. "With business Jack and I agree on most things but argue it out when we don't. I agree with his decisions ninety percent of the time. I consider him brilliant."

She could only imagine what he would say next, maybe confirm her thoughts that Jack had some kind of nefarious plans and that like usual he agreed with his father. "But," Keary said at last, "you are here so we can all meet each other on a personal level, and Jack can get to know you as such. I'm sure he wants to be a part of his grandson's life, and you come along with that."

She hadn't yet let go of her annoyance at how Jack summoned her and didn't give her a chance to decide when she would come. Keary had gone along with it as well. "You're sure that's what it is? Maybe it's not that he's interested in me because he wants his grandson to be a part of his life. Maybe it's to get into my head and see where I am? How many times have we heard that in the meetings?"

"Do you blame him?" He seemed to watch steadily for her answer. "One night together, and you're pregnant."

"And I'm nobody."

"I didn't say that, Zacari."

"You didn't have to."

He ran a hand through his hair. "I'll talk to you later at dinner. I just wanted to let you know I'm on your side. No one here will make you feel like you're not welcome or you're somehow less than we are as you seem to think."

He leaned forward as if to kiss her but thought better of it and walked out. Zacari shut the door behind him, careful not to slam it and let him know how this situation affected her. Anyway, her words and attitude had made that abundantly clear.

Zacari unlocked her suitcase and pulled one blouse from the pile. Too sleepy to do more than that, she shoved the bag aside and flopped on the bed. Before she could consider all that had happened or what to wear to dinner, she fell into a dreamless sleep.

Chapter Nine

Zacari stepped from the shower, dried herself, and then pulled on a simple blouse and stretchy maternity jeans. After struggling into knee-highs, she pushed her feet into a pair of mules and left her room. Keary was just coming down the hall, and he paused in front of her.

"Perfect timing. Are you ready?"

She nodded. He took her hand, giving it a gentle squeeze. Zacari looked up at him, and the encouraging expression on his face warmed her heart to him. "Thanks for staying by me in this," she whispered.

He drew her close. Zacari's heart beat thumped hard in her chest. Her lips parted, drawing Keary's eyes to them. He lowered his head. The kiss was fleeting, but it ignited a fire in her that she wanted only him to extinguish. Forget the meeting. Forget the dinner. Just let him hold her this way and make love to her.

"We should go downstairs," he mouthed against her cheek.

She didn't want to, but she let him help her down the stairs and into the living room. Jack sat on a couch holding a drink, and his wife was curled next to him. When Zacari and Keary entered, they both stood up.

Claudia smiled. "How was your nap, Zacari? I hope you feel rested after your flight. I can only imagine how tiring it must be carrying a baby." When she said the words, Zacari had the impression Claudia had never been pregnant before, but she didn't detect sadness or regret.

"Like nobody's business," Zacari agreed. "The more he grows, the more he seems to sit on my bladder, and I feel like I have to go to the bathroom all the time."

Jack's eyes widened. "*He*?"

Zacari shifted her attention to Jack. "Yes, the baby's a boy. I have a picture from the last sonogram if you'd like so see. My...*our* son seems to be really proud of himself, so it wasn't hard to find out that he was a boy."

Claudia laughed. "Oh yes, an O'Connor man." Apparently she didn't catch Zacari's slip up or Jack's reaction to it. Zacari didn't look at Keary. The fact was she'd been calling her son *her* baby for six months while Keary wasn't there, and breaking the habit didn't come that easily. No doubt Jack was reading all kinds of evidence into it.

When they were settled at the dinner table, and Claudia had laid out the delicious looking meal, Jack didn't waste a minute getting to the point. "Zacari, you must know that I have concerns regarding the baby? Such as are you sure it's Keary's?"

Claudia's fork clattered to her plate. Keary swore, and Zacari just sat there with her mouth open. She'd heard Jack light into his executives at work. Not once did he raise his voice, and he really didn't reprimand the lower orders. He'd talk to their supervisor and let them handle it. Jeb had once told her that was Jack's way of respecting the chain of command and setting an example for everyone else to follow. He didn't raise his voice now or seem unpleasant exactly. But like when she'd overheard him by chance talking to an executive about a problem, his gentle inquiries held the power to slice a person and make them feel like they'd gotten something wrong and they better fix it quick. No one's life depended on getting the situation straight, but it *felt* like it. That was another of Jack's gifts.

"That's not your concern. Zacari and I have cleared that up," Keary assured him, but they hadn't. Keary never even brought up the subject. Debbie claimed Keary would demand a paternity test.

Jack waved a hand in Keary's direction. "I don't doubt you for a second, son."

"Meaning you doubt me," Zacari snapped. All she wanted to do was throw her fork down and storm out, but that was like admitting she had something to hide or was doing something wrong. "With all due respect, Jack, I'm not a whore that sleeps around and doesn't know who the father of my baby is. Now maybe I'll lose my job for talking to you like this, but Keary's right, it's none of your damn business."

"Whoa, whoa," Jack said. "I'm not accusing you of anything, Zacari. And what we say here has no bearing on your job. You are excellent at what you do. This time is just for us all to get to know each other, and I'm sure you'll agree, getting all our cards out on the table is the best way to move forward."

She bit her lip. For all the time she'd known Jack, she couldn't read what he was thinking or feeling. She had only her preconceived notions to go on, and it was hard letting them go with the first question like that. If Jack or Keary insisted, would she get a paternity test? Would she be offended? *Hell yeah I would.*

"It's not an unreasonable question," Jack continued.

"Maybe we should wait until after dinner to discuss this," Claudia suggested. "Upsetting Zacari while she's eating can't be good for the baby or her."

Zacari smiled at Claudia, but it was pretty much too late. She'd lost her appetite. The only reason she shoveled a few bites into her mouth was for the baby. The bagel from this morning was long gone, along with the trail mix she always carried in her purse for snack attacks.

Jack didn't seem inclined to let the subject drop, but he gave in anyway. That was different. He always got the last word, and everyone bowed to his wishes. But this was home, and a man could rule a corporation all he wanted, but the woman he chose to marry often ran the show here. Keary found herself liking Claudia all the more. After dinner, she helped Claudia clear away the dishes, while the men headed into another room. Zacari rinsed and handed Claudia each dish as she piled them into the dishwasher.

"Stop worrying," Claudia said when they had remained silent for a while.

"I'm not."

"You are," she insisted. "You love him, and make no mistake if I can see it, Jack can too. For a man, he's very perceptive. It freaked me out and annoyed the hell out of me when we were dating." She laughed. "I thought he might be gay."

Zacari had at first squirmed at Claudia saying she

loved Keary, but then she burst out laughing. "As if only gay men can be sensitive? I've never thought of Jack that way, but I guess he'd have to be to be able to read frickin' everyone the way he does. I don't think I've met anyone like him."

"Jack or Keary?"

"Both." She sighed. In retrospect, her ex-friend Pam had been so vain Zacari couldn't share the hard stuff with her, so she didn't know how to relate to Claudia now. And it wasn't like the older woman was her mother-in-law. The way Claudia's eyes shined with pride and love when she talked about Jack, she wasn't going to admit her real feelings. For all she knew, Claudia might go back and tell Jack everything she said. "I like Keary. I admire Jack for his brilliance, but he's not going to orchestrate me and my son's lives like he controls everything at work. I came here this time, but I won't be summoned again."

Claudia dried her hands on a towel and patted Zacari's shoulder. "I understand. But what I was getting at saying Jack knows you love Keary is to say that while he can see it, he will evaluate whether he thinks you're good for Keary. Do you know why Keary calls his father by his name?"

Zacari shrugged.

"Because they've always been more like close friends than anything else. They're a lot alike." She laughed. "Keary's sister Karen calls Jack Daddy, but I don't think Keary has since he was eight or nine." She tapped her lip. "I guess you know their biological mother died when Keary was five. Maybe that's what drew them close. Then I came along when Karen was three and Keary was seven. They're my babies, and I love them very much.

"Keary has his father's temperament, never raises his voice, is kind but firm in what he wants. He has rarely found a reason to oppose his father, and if he does, they haggle it out. Keary seems satisfied that your baby is his, and he will make that known to Jack. So, you don't have to worry. Jack will come to respect Keary's decisions regarding this situation."

Zacari shook her head. "It's funny, on the outside, it looks different. I thought Keary just did whatever Jack wanted him to."

Claudia's eyes widened. "A weak-willed man? Oh no no, my dear, Keary has his own mind. I'm sure you'll see that before long. Well we better get in there before they think you ran away."

Zacari stiffened her back. "I've never run away from anyone, and I'm not about to now."

Claudia winked. "I didn't think you would."

The two of them went to the living room where Jack and Claudia had waited before dinner. Keary and Jack stood up when they walked in, and Jack held out a hand to Claudia. She drifted with gentle grace into the crook of his arm, and Zacari's heart ached to have the obvious love they shared. The three years she'd lived with Melvin, she still felt lonely. It was just after she caught him cheating that she realized they'd never truly loved each other.

"Zacari," Jack began, "what do your parents think about the baby? Are they supportive?"

She stiffened. Keary turned to look at her. They'd never discussed her lack of family, so he didn't know any more than his father did. Now that she knew Keary had his father, his stepmother, and a sister, she felt all the more alone. Not one single person in this world was truly on her side. She realized now that's what had made Pam's betrayal all the more devastating. Was she that blind to the way people were, or was she destined to be walk alone?

"I never really knew my mother. She left my father and I when I was two. My father died of cancer when I was seventeen. As far as I know, I don't have any other family." At some point, she rested her hand on her belly without thinking. Zacari would show her son all the love in her heart. She'd never leave him, and she'd support him in whatever he did in life.

"I'm sorry to hear that," Jack said with a genuine inflection in his tone. "Shall we sit?"

Jack and Claudia sat close side-by-side, but Zacari chose to put a little space between Keary and herself. She didn't need his father to think she was weezling her way into their pockets. With that in mind, she decided to take a card from Jack's book and be direct.

"I know the thought that maybe I got pregnant on purpose is running through all of your heads. I can deny it, but I have no proof. My life and what I do will prove the kind of person I am." She drew in a deep breath and found that her hands shook a little. Clutching them together in her lap, she continued. "I don't want your money. I've already told Keary I don't expect a thing from him. He doesn't even have to be there."

Keary frowned. "And I told you, that I will be there. Period. You already know what it's like for a parent to leave you. I know you don't want that for our son."

She gasped. All this time, she hadn't thought of that. How could she not? Yet, she'd only been thinking about herself and her own resolve. Of course if Keary wasn't in her son's life, her baby would question it at some point and feel the hurt and loss, especially when he looked around and saw other kids with their father present.

"I never considered that," she whispered.

"It's something you should think of," Jack commented. "I didn't raise Keary to shirk his responsibilities. You must accept that he will be a part of the child's life. It's the right thing to do."

Not because he loved the baby, but because it was right. Zacari hated these complications and the second guessing what everyone said. Her son didn't deserve this either, but only time would straighten it all out, that and Zacari letting them know what she'd tolerate and what she wouldn't if it got out of hand.

Jack placed a hand on his wife's knee, squeezed, and then stood up. "Good that part is settled." He crossed to tea tray on wheels which she hadn't noticed before. Several bottles of alcohol, glasses, and a bucket of ice sat on its surface. After asking Claudia and Keary what they wanted to drink, he made them and then brought Zacari a glass of orange juice.

"Of course you don't drink," he said. The words didn't even resemble a question.

"No, I don't. Thanks." She took the glass and sipped from it.

"Another point I wanted to make," Jack continued, "was I understand you two weren't in a relationship when this happened. You realize you and Keary don't have to be together for you two to be involved with the child's development?"

Her eyebrow shot up. She clenched her jaw but didn't

say a word. Keary grunted, "Jack."

Jack's smile didn't waver. "It's a simple question, son." He paused waiting for her answer.

She took her time draining her orange juice and then sat the glass down on a nearby table. When she slid to the edge of her seat, Keary rose to help her stand. She faced Jack head on since he hadn't moved away after he handed her the drink. "I get it, okay. You're not happy with this situation. You're used to running the show, telling everybody where to go and what to do. You're under the impression that you're going to tell me in my personal life what I can and can't do. But you are *so* wrong. If I sleep with your son again, I won't be telling you about it or getting your permission. This meeting is over. I'm leaving in the morning. Claudia, good night."

Jack waited until Zacari was at the door and Keary had opened it before he spoke again. "I wanted to have Claudia take you shopping while you were in town. I'm sure you won't deny my wife that pleasure?"

Zacari stopped and closed her eyes. Earlier, she'd picked up on the fact that Claudia had never been pregnant, but with her sweet spirit and the excitement she showed about the baby, Zacari guessed the older woman would love to shop for baby items.

"Oh, my goodness, that would be so much fun!" Claudia exclaimed. "We could do lunch afterward or before, and I know the best stores to visit in Manhattan."

How the heck could she say no to that? Keary moved in close to her, and his breath stirred a tendril of her hair. He rested a hand at the small of her back. "If you want to go, I will take you. You do not have to feel like you're obligated. Whatever you want, Zacari."

She glanced up at him. His expression showed kindness, but was he reading her to know she wouldn't say no to Claudia who'd done nothing to offend her? Would he go against what Jack wanted should she resist? After all, he'd come at the summons too.

"Fine," she said. "I'll stay one more day."

"Great." Jack approached her. "I'll arrange for—"

"Claudia and I can make the arrangements on our own, thanks. Good night." This time she didn't wait for him to say more. She hurried out with Keary at her side. He walked with her up to her room and stopped outside her door.

"You seem determined to antagonize him." He grinned.

She put a hand on her hip. "Well I'm not bowing to his every wish, that's for sure."

"I hope you're not insinuating that I am."

She shrugged. "If the shoe fits…"

Keary lifted her chin. "If I said I want to make you my wife, what would you say to that?"

Her eyes widened. She stumbled back a step, but Keary reached out to steady her. She shook her head. "You're only saying that because…I have no idea why you're saying that. It's crazy."

"Why?"

"Because a little while ago you were about to start a thing with Debbie. I can't imagine those feelings have flown out the door with finding out about our son."

She thought she saw a flash of guilt, but it was gone before she could be sure. "Don't bring her into this."

"Why not? There's a lot between us."

He tsked. "There's nothing between us." He took a

step closer and leaned down to kiss her. Zacari couldn't help tilting her head back and letting him slip his tongue into her mouth. A craving to feel him inside of her made her sway into his arms. He slid his hands along her sides to her hips, but when he would have cupped her pussy, she stopped him.

"I need to get to sleep. Something tells me running around with Claudia will wear me out, and I need all the energy I can get."

Worry etched his handsome face, but the tropical sea that was his eye color had darkened with his desire. "Don't do too much. I don't want you wearing yourself out."

"Yes, Daddy." She smirked and slipped into her room. The last she saw of Keary as she shut the door was of him adjusting his slacks. Zacari calling him Daddy was a real turn-on for him. It was for her too. She panted with her back against the door, knowing she'd have to take a cooler shower than normal if she was going to get any sleep.

Chapter Ten

Keary stood at his room's window and watched Zacari get into the car with his stepmother. He had no idea why he'd blurt out that stuff about making her his wife. Maybe he wanted to prove to her he wasn't dangling from his father's puppet strings. Many had made that mistake in the past because he and Jack saw eye-to-eye on many issues. Yet, when he said it, he'd only ended up looking like the boy she must think of him—the boy trying to prove he was a man.

He sighed and rubbed the back of his neck. True she provoked him with the outrageous things she said, the way she was direct and spoke her mind. He admired it, was often amused by it. The fact that he knew Zacari had that type of personality made him believe she wasn't the type to pull a trick to get money. Keary had always been an excellent judge of character.

On the heels of Zacari pulling out, another vehicle rolled into the driveway. Keary guessed it was Jeb and Debbie. That fact was confirmed a moment later when a long, slender leg came into view followed by the rest of

Debbie's beautiful form. He waited for the interest in his body to stir, but it remained dormant. Not like last night when he'd almost picked Zacari up and carried her into her room to make mad passionate love to her. So maybe his feelings weren't conflicted at all. He wanted Zacari.

Of course she would take some convincing, but he would bring her around and show her this wasn't about the baby—or not just about the baby. He'd spend time with her, get to know her and let her know him. Keary was pretty sure Zacari didn't notice the loss and pain she'd displayed when she mentioned her parents. He would do all he could to change her experiences for the better. The first step was to be clear about Debbie. He would let Debbie know there was no chance they would develop something between them and show Zacari that he'd chosen her and wanted no one else.

* * * *

Keary reviewed the data Jack slid down the table to him. He nodded after a while. "I have to agree this looks good. I am surprised after our meeting that Eve would be this generous."

"Hm, but she said she'd already had it written up, remember?" Debbie put in.

He glanced at her and noted the jealousy. He needed to speak with her before Zacari got back, but Jack had dragged him into the work they were doing, and it had consumed their time over the last few hours. Keary had found it hard to concentrate worried about Zacari and if she was wearing herself out.

After glancing at his watch and seeing that it was just

past four in the afternoon, he dropped the papers on the table and stood up. "Will you excuse me just a moment?" He didn't wait for anyone to respond, but he walked out of the room and down the hall a few steps. He tugged his phone from his pocket and speed-dialed Zacari.

She answered on the third ring out of breath. "Hello?"

"Why are you breathing so hard," he demanded, a little more roughly than he intended. "Don't you think you've been gone long enough, Zacari? I thought you said you wouldn't overdo it."

She laughed. "I don't remember saying that. Anyway, I was breathing hard because Claudia and I almost ran to beat another woman for this amazing antique crib. Wait until you see it. It's awesome."

"Ran?"

"Lord, man, get a grip. You know good and well I did not really run with this belly. I wobbled faster than usual. But I got it." She paused to catch her breath. "And stop grumbling. We'll be back soon. You act like you missed me."

"I did."

She didn't respond.

"Zacari?"

"The baby is fine, Keary. You don't have to worry. We're leaving to come back now. I can't believe the amount of stuff I let Claudia buy. But there's tons more I said no to. Anyway, we'll be there soon."

He was about to explain that it wasn't just the baby he was worried about, but she said good-bye and disconnected the call. He growled and stuffed his phone back into his pocket. After he had rejoined the meeting, he remembered that he hadn't told her Debbie was present at his father's house.

He sighed and threw his attention for the time being into work. Not that he should even be involved in this project, but since he was here, Jack pulled him in to get his impressions of their plans. At first Keary questioned if Jack was trying to wedge a monkey wrench between him and Zacari, but then he knew his father. Jack would be straight forward. He knew how his father thought. If anything came between Keary and Zacari, then they weren't meant for a stronger relationship. That would be Jack's view, and nothing he did to manipulate the situation in either direction would change that. His tactic would be discussion, long after everyone was fed up with talking. Probably why he got the last word in every situation.

Jeb answered a call, spoke a few minutes, and then hung up. "I'm going to have to make a run for an hour or so, but I will be back."

"No, go ahead," Jack encouraged him. "I know your grandmother isn't doing too well. If you need to spend the rest of the night with your family, do. We can pick this up in the morning."

Jeb uttered a grateful sigh. "Thanks, Jack. It's a good thing that I'm back here. My mother isn't taking this so well, and she's not a young woman anymore."

Jack waved a hand. "Family comes first. That has always been my policy." Keary had to agree. Jack had never stood in the way of anyone who had a legitimate need at home. Early on their company policy had been set to allow new mothers to have extra time at home with newborns. The word had gotten around the industry along with other incentives, so they were never without quality candidates for open positions.

The doorbell rang after Jeb left, and Jack went to answer leaving Keary alone with Debbie. He figured his father would be a while since he'd ordered dinner to be catered tonight. Keary decided now might be a good time to speak with Debbie.

"I wanted to talk to you about our relationship," he began.

She looked up from the paper she was reading, her cheeks pinking. Debbie was a beautiful woman, but there still was no reaction in him other than acknowledging the truth. He stood and moved to take the chair next to her.

"We don't really have a relationship. We spoke over the phone, flirted a little, and exchanged a ton of instant messages." If possible she grew redder. "Many very spicy."

That was true. They might not have slept together, but the messages had amounted to Internet sex, or close to it. He'd been stuck practically in the desert. She was a lifeline to home. In some ways, their closeness came about from the fact that she was there. It could have been anyone else.

He placed a hand over hers. "I don't want you to think I was using you or that I'm just throwing you aside now."

She averted her eyes. Keary hoped he didn't see wetness glistening on her lashes as she blinked it away. "My mind tells me you didn't. My heart feels differently. The truth is, I fell for you. I know long distance relationships are tricky, and a lot can be inferred that wasn't there. It's my fault. I don't blame you."

Guilt racked Keary's being. Could this get any more

complicated? "I'm sorry. I never meant to hurt you. It's just that..." I want Zacari. *I've wanted her from the moment I saw her.*

Not at the bar. He'd met her in the office at one of his father's meetings. He'd surreptitiously watched her, the way she moved and gestured with her hands, the tone of her voice. Keary had been surprised when his father called on an assistant for her opinion of one of their accounts, but then he agreed with the decision later. Zacari was one of the most down to earth women he'd ever met. She'd admitted that the plans were pretentious, that the average Joe or Jane wouldn't respond to their media campaign. That was when Keary was hooked, he decided.

And she'd only drawn him in more after their night of passion.

Realizing that he'd been daydreaming about Zacari, he snapped his attention back to Debbie. "Like I said, I don't want to hurt you anymore than I have, but I think it's clear what we intended is not going to happen. I'm sorry."

"You don't have to see her, you know," Debbie said. Resentment dripped from her words.

Keary lowered his brows. He could accept Jack's comments about his personal life because that's how his father was, and Keary knew he'd do just what he wanted in the end. But Debbie had no right and no business giving her opinion. "Pardon?"

"Accident or not, she got pregnant. But you don't have to throw your life away because of *her* baby." She grasped his arm, her eyes swimming with unshed tears. "I know you. You'll always do what's right, but you and her together isn't right."

Keary surged to his feet. For something to do with his hands and a way to work off some of his anger, he jerked his suit jacket closed and fastened the three buttons. "What Zacari and I have is none of your business, and if you ever give the impression that somehow my son is inferior because of who his mother is, you will regret it."

Debbie bit her bottom lip while her eyes widened so much, they must hurt. He knew she'd realized she made a mistake. When he would have turned away, she grabbed onto his arm. "I'm so sorry. I never meant to imply that. Forgive me."

The door burst open. "Keary, isn't this outfit cute?"

Zacari stopped cold. Her shocked gaze slid from Keary to Debbie and back again. He knew in that instant that no one had told her Debbie was here. That had been his place given what almost happened between them, and he had failed. Worse, Debbie was standing too close to him with deep rose lips from biting them in her embarrassment. With the color in her cheeks, anyone would think she'd just been kissed. At least, he could read the conclusion in Zacari's expression.

She took an unsteady step back. "I'm sorry to interrupt."

She stuffed the light blue baby outfit which he'd gotten a glimpse of back into the bag hanging from her arm. When she whirled to leave, Keary pulled out of Debbie's grasp and followed her, slamming the door behind him.

"Zacari, wait," he called when she'd put a little distance between them.

"No, it's fine," she called over her shoulder. "I

thought since Jack was in the dining room directing the caterer that you weren't meeting. I wanted to show you what I bought. I knew Jeb was here but not Debbie."

She rambled on until she got to the stairs, but he closed the space between them and took hold of her arm. "Wait. You were not interrupting. I was telling Debbie there can't be anything between us. I meant also to tell you she was coming for Jack's meeting."

"You meant to?" Zacari rolled her eyes. "Whatever, Keary. You do what you want. Let me go. I said I didn't mean to interrupt you. I'm going to bed."

"Not without eating." He took her bag from her and glanced around the foyer. Several more waited to be taken up. He'd get them after he helped her to her room. "If you prefer to eat in your room, that's okay, but you can't skip a meal. And don't tell me you and my mom ate dinner out, because she's the one who made the catering arrangements at Jack's request."

Zacari had put one foot on the step but then drew it back and faced him. "You think you can tell me what I can and cannot do?"

"If it affects your health, yes." He wasn't backing down. He knew she was upset about what she thought she saw, and something told him Zacari would spite herself to get away from him. She needed to eat, and he'd make sure she did even if he came off as overbearing.

She stood staring at him, eyes narrowed, lips pursed. Anger radiated off of her smooth brown skin, but all he wanted to do was to caress her until she let it all go and purred for him. He allowed his gaze to linger on her lips remembering their soft sweetness, and then he trailed downward. Her dress at the neckline was cut low, allowing for a glimpse of her full breasts. Keary hadn't tasted her nipples since that night when he sampled her milk, and he found himself craving more.

She must have noticed how his cock hardened and the way he couldn't remove his focus from her breasts. Hands balled into fists at her sides and pretending she had no reaction whatsoever, she turned and stomped up the steps. Keary fell into step behind her and gave her support when she needed it. He followed her into her bedroom and laid her bags on the bed. Within a few minutes, he had gone back downstairs for the rest and brought those up as well.

Zacari stood near the bed arms crossed and still angry at him. "That's all. You can go."

He ignored her and began searching through the bag she'd come into the meeting with. He pulled out a light blue outfit that looked similar to a sailor's uniform but made of heavier material. Keary glanced at the tag. Velour onesie with front pockets. It cost a hundred and ten dollars. His eyebrows rose.

"I know it's expensive," she lamented, taking it from him and folding it with care. "Babies grow out of this stuff so fast, but Claudia fell in love with it. Trust me, I did not let her get much more in that store. I mean this is Armani! I had no idea they even made stuff for babies. It doesn't make sense."

She rambled again, not meeting his eyes. Keary pulled the garment from her and tugged her close to him. He expected her to resist or pull away, but she let him hold her. Desire flamed to life inside him, and all he could think of was stripping her naked and taking her until she cried out his name.

"I want you," he told her and waited for her response.

Zacari met his eyes for a fleeting moment, and then she stared at his chest. She played with the button on his shirt, seeming to try to figure out what she should do. Should she reject him or accept what he wanted. Keary imagined she hadn't believed a word he said about Debbie, and he didn't blame her. But how could he settle her mind? How could he prove that he wasn't like that other bastard?

"Zacari, did you hear me?" he asked when she didn't answer.

"Yes."

"And?" He traced a path with his thumb down her back. She shivered in his arms, and he longed to mold her body with his. But that would hurt her, and he never wanted to do that. "You want me. I feel it in the way you tremble at my touch."

He demonstrated by running the backs of his fingers over her bare skin. Just looking at it turned him on. The contrast of her mocha tone to his paler but tanned skin pleased him. He never thought it would, but then maybe it was the fact that this was Zacari and not any woman. He had no desire to go find another black woman to test the attraction. Zacari was what he wanted.

Keary lowered his head and found her lips for the second time. Darting his tongue into her mouth, he reached around and grabbed a handful of her rounded rear and squeezed. His cock shifted in his pants. She moaned. Not waiting for any more of an invitation than that, he backed her to the bed and placed gentle pressure on her shoulders to make her sit down.

After he got her to lie prostrate, he skimmed his hands

over her thighs while watching her face. Her bottom lip caught between her teeth. It took all he had to remain where he was, kneeling between her legs, not to go up there and rescue that sweet lip and take it between his own. As it was, Keary had no doubt what he was about to do would be just as good.

When he reached her panties beneath her dress, Zacari put a hand over his to still him. "Keary, what are you doing?"

"What do you think I'm doing?" he countered.

"I-I..."

A shudder passed over her, leaving goose bumps in their wake. At the angle he was, Keary could smell her excitement. He guessed when he explored farther, he'd find her soaking wet and ready for his tongue. Mouth watering in anticipation, he hurried to lower her panties. At that point, Zacari quaked, and she fought not to cry out. He grinned watching her fail to hide her own anxiousness.

"You want this," he said.

"You always say that as if you're telling me what I want."

"Am I wrong?" Keary paused after he'd removed her panties and held them up in one hand. A questioning expression on his face, he waited. Doubts and fears flickered in her lovely eyes, touching him, but there wasn't much he could change. She had to accept his explanation or push him away. He prayed it wouldn't be the latter.

"No," she said at last, and Keary let go of the breath he'd held. "You're not wrong. I want it. I want *you*."

"Then I'm going to eat your pussy," he announced.

"Do you object to that?"

She groaned and closed her eyes. "Do you have to talk so dirty before you do anything? You're making me hotter."

Keary chuckled. He pushed one thigh aside and licked the tender skin. Zacari squirmed. He raised the other leg and caressed it with the tip of his tongue as well. His lover arched up off the bed. Keary watched her pussy clench, calling to him in silence. Her thick white cream gathered, all ready for him to lick it up. Rather than rush things, Keary spread her legs wider so he could enjoy the view more.

"Do you know how wet you are, baby?" He leaned in to blow on her softness. She bunched the sheets under a fist and pressed the other hand against her mouth. Keary reached up and dragged the hand down to her side. "Tell me you want me to eat you."

"Damn it, Keary, you know I want it," she complained.

"Say it."

She bit off a scream. Keary squeezed the backs of her thighs. He massaged her soft skin all the way up to her pussy but didn't touch her most sensitive area. Instead, he blew on it again. Her core pulsed. More cream descended. He ached to lick up every drop, but held back.

For a few moments longer, they were at odds, but Keary knew she would give into him. Half of Zacari's pleasure was in his taking control. He couldn't wait for the time when she would give birth and then later. He had plans to take her in ways she only imagined, and show her how far he was willing to go to please them both. They had experienced a little of it that night in the limo, but there was so much more.

"Eat me," she pleaded. "Please, Daddy, eat my pussy."

Keary fell forward to rest his cheek on her thigh. For a second, he came close to release. He had to suck in and blow out several breaths to calm himself when she called him Daddy in that throaty voice, all sultry and sexual. If he thought he was in control, Zacari proved him wrong. Keary would bend over backward for her when she called him Daddy.

Snaking his tongue out, he began to scoop up her sweet cream. He groaned and let the sound vibrate through her pussy. Zacari cried out. Keary started at the base, teasing the thin pink membrane and then worked his way higher. He dipped his tongue briefly into her tight opening to ladle more of her essence, but then he withdrew and continued on. All the time, Zacari twisted her hips so he had to hold her down.

Growing hungrier, he ate her with more enthusiasm. He closed his mouth over her clit and sucked it hard. Zacari screamed and then stuffed a pillow against her face. Her cries and the quivers in her thigh muscles let him know she was near an orgasm. He concentrated on her bud while sticking a finger up her channel. When he spun to the side to angle over her hip, he added two more fingers and worked them in and out of her while he laved her clit.

Zacari's hips rose and then fell. She panted and whined his name, begging him to stop in one breath and then urging him on with the next. Keary had no intention of backing off. He knew his baby needed what he was giving her, to ease her tension, to make her forget everyone else but him. Only when she let out a muffled shout with her release did he work her through and then sat up.

His lover lay panting, her big breasts rising and falling, mesmerizing him. He licked his lips, tasting her juices. While he stared at his cocoa goddess, his cock strained in his pants. He imagined her full lips wrapped around it bringing him to an urgent and violent climax. Aching need shook him, but he suppressed the desire. Not for a few months would he get the satisfaction of that, but he would get it. He damn sure *would* get it.

When he didn't reach for her again, Zacari opened her eyes and looked at him. "Aren't you going to finish it? I know you must want to come."

"Of course I do, but you're tired. You've had a long day." He rose from the bed prepared to go downstairs and make her a plate of food. "Get your things ready for your bath. I'm going to get you something to eat, and then when you finish, I'll help you take a bath."

She pushed herself to her elbow. "Are you serious? I can see you're hard as a rock. Keary, I can take you."

"No."

He could almost see the thought as it slid into her mind. Zacari thought he wasn't going to take his release with her because he planned to get it with Debbie. She schooled her features and glanced away. The tension between them that had drained away after he pleasured her, came back with a vengeance. Keary suppressed a sigh.

"I don't need your help with my bath," she told him. "I'll take a shower."

He didn't feel like arguing. "I'll be right back with

your food."

Keary hurried through making Zacari's plate. He didn't want her to relax so much that she fell asleep and didn't eat. Not bothering to answer more than a few questions about where she was and if he would join his family, Keary hurried upstairs. When he opened Zacari's door, she paused in the act of placing a nightgown on the bed next to a few other toiletries.

"You could knock," she snapped. "We're not married."

He shut the door and placed her plate on the nightstand. Without saying a word, he ran her bath and added salts she'd placed there. The scent of lavender filled the bathroom.

"I said I'm not taking a bath," she yelled.

"And I said I'm helping you," he answered. He went back to the room and turned her to face him with his hands on her shoulders. "You can fight me night and day. I've made my decision. I'm going to be here for you."

She frowned. "By force?"

"If necessary."

"You're the most egoistical, stubborn, pain in my ass man I have ever met!" she ranted. "I suppose if I refuse to eat, you'll feed me too, won't you?"

Keary smiled and kissed the top of her head. "I'm glad we understand each other. Now, eat up before it gets cold. If you're a good girl, I might even rub your feet before I put you to bed."

Zacari grumbled, but he saw the smile she tried to hide. For six months, she had stood alone. Keary wasn't letting that happen ever again. Zacari could either embrace it or battle him all the way. His resolve stood.

Chapter Eleven

Zacari woke to bad news, and tears flooded her eyes. "Damaged?" she cried. "Why? How can the crib be damaged?" This couldn't be. She'd fought for that antique crib, and it was the only other expensive item she'd let Claudia buy. The piece was one of a kind and in mint condition, or it had been yesterday.

"I'm so sorry, Miss Lamont. The men who assist me have never done this before, and I suspect that the leg might have been week in the first place. I promise we are making the necessary repairs, but I want you to come down here and see for yourself. If it doesn't meet with your approval, by all means, you will receive a full refund."

"I don't want a refund. I want my crib!"

A light knock sounded on the door, and Keary walked in. By that time, tears were streaming down her cheeks. Zacari rushed to scrub them away not wanting him to see. She knew she was being unreasonable, but yet again, the emotions were out of control. One look at Zacari's face, and Keary rushed forward, took her into his arms, and whipped the phone from her hand.

"Who is this?" he demanded. When he paused, Zacari assumed the elderly shop owner was filling him in. Keary's face creased in anger. "We will be there in less than an hour. I'm sure this will be resolved in a way that will make Zacari happy."

After he hung up, he lifted her chin and kissed her. "Get dressed. I will take you. I'll straighten it all out."

"But…" She didn't bother arguing. Once Keary got a notion in his head that was it. All of a sudden, she was less worried about getting the crib and more concerned that Keary wouldn't upset the old woman.

He strolled to the door like she'd just fall in line with his plans. She half expected the man to pick out her clothes, but he just winked and left the happiest person on the planet. Zacari figured out that Keary got a kick out of bailing her out of messes. Maybe that's what all men were like. They needed to be needed. She shook her head and rolled her eyes before getting dressed. Let him do it. Whatever, it saved her a headache.

True to Keary's word, they arrived at the shop in less than an hour, and on top of that, Keary got the whole situation cleared up. Before Zacari knew what was happening they were back on the street, and she blew out a relieved breath.

"I can't believe you got that straightened out so fast," she told him, knowing she was grinning up at him like a lovesick idiot. Hopefully, he couldn't tell. "And you didn't upset the lady."

He chuckled. "You make it sound like I'm an ogre. Have you ever seen me bully old ladies?"

Zacari laughed. "No, I guess not. My bad. You're my

hero."

An odd expression settled over his handsome face. She wondered what wheels were turning behind his eyes, but the look was gone in an instant. Zacari didn't know what drew her attention away from Keary at that moment since she loved looking at him, listening to him speak, and feeling his touch. But all of a sudden, it felt like someone was staring at her, and she glanced around. At first she didn't spot anyone familiar even though she was back in her hometown.

"Do you know her?" Keary asked.

She turned in the direction he pointed his chin and was surprised to see Pam standing on the opposite side of the street. The way she aimed a look of pure hatred Zacari's way was so palpable, Keary stood a little in front of her as if to protect her from it.

Melvin stepped out of a shop behind Pam, and without even letting the man get his bearings, Pam dragged him into the street headed Zacari's way. Her stomach knotted. She was so not in the mood for the drama Pam was obviously bringing.

"Oh my goodness, girl, Zacari, I knew that was you. You look so different," Pam gushed. She squinted eyes overdone with makeup and false eyelashes. "Did you put on weight?"

"Stop it, Pam," Melvin said and pulled at her arm. She jerked it free.

"I'm sure you can clearly see, I'm pregnant," Zacari told her.

"Baby, who is this?" Keary asked, not to be ignored. He rested his hand on her lower back.

Zacari hesitated and then thought what did she have

to feel funny about. Keary knew about her past, at least where these two were concerned. And it was for sure she had nothing whatsoever to be ashamed about regarding Keary. "Keary, this is my ex, Melvin and..." She started to say the skank he decided to leave her for, but she changed her mind. That would be sinking to their level. "And this is Pam."

Keary eyed Melvin. "*This* is him?"

She could have kissed him the way he made it sound like Melvin was not worthy to acknowledge, let alone to cry over. If Melvin could have paled under his dark brown skin, he would have. His nostrils flared, and his lips tightened at the obvious insult.

Pam put her hands on her hips. Her nails were freshly done with tips and designs. Her hair was in perfect order. At least they weren't hurting any from the designer handbag she held. Then again maybe that business deal she'd warned them about wasn't going as expected. Pam looked like she was spending whatever Melvin made, while he wore obviously worn out shoes and slacks that had been pressed one too many times. That was never Melvin. If nothing else, he'd always been well put together.

"And who is he?" Pam demanded like it was any of her business.

"Keary O'Connor," Zacari stated. And at that moment, no words were needed to qualify him any further, because their limo rolled up to the curb to pick them up. Zacari had complained that she didn't need to travel every-frickin'-where in the limo, but Keary had explained that parking wouldn't be found easily, and he didn't want to leave her on the sidewalk alone while he went to retrieve the car from wherever he found a space. His insistence that having a driver was better. Now with jealousy pouring off of Pam, her expression was priceless.

Zacari couldn't resist calling over her shoulder in a saccharin-y sweet voice, "You two have a nice day. Good seeing you."

In the back of the limo, Keary scooted her close to his side and wrapped an arm around her. She settled her head on his shoulder.

"Okay?" he said.

She nodded. "Yes, I'm fine." She glanced up at him, and he kissed her. "You know you're special, right?"

His eyebrows went up. "Am I?"

"Yes, you are. Very much so."

* * * *

Three months later

Zacari slipped out of bed, trying not to wake Keary. For the last few months, he'd been constantly at her side, taking care of her, making sure she didn't have one need or even desire that went unfulfilled. Every day she loved him more and more, but the fear that he did all this for their son remained. She didn't have any real worries about Debbie or any other woman in his life at this point—especially since he was always with her, and when he wasn't he called to check up on her. The man drove her insane sometimes treating her like she was made of glass. But even that made her crazy about him.

She padded to the kitchen and opened the refrigerator. The bag of chips Keary had been munching on earlier called her name, but every time she ate just one chip, heartburn kicked her butt bad.

A half of one can't hurt.

The bag landed in her hand some kind of way, and she found herself munching down on a handful. "Oh crap."

She rolled the bag up and stuffed it back into the refrigerator. Just when she did, liquid ran down her leg. She stood there staring at the puddle on the floor, stupidly wondering if she'd just peed on herself.

The kitchen door opened, and Keary strolled in yawning. He stretched thickly muscled arms over his head, drawing her attention. "What are you doing up, Zacari? Midnight craving?"

"I..." She glanced back down at the floor, and then the first contraction hit—hard. She doubled over in pain and cried out.

"Zacari!" Keary was at her side in an instant. His eyes wide, he laid a hand on her belly. "What's wrong? Come here and sit down."

"Oh no," she whimpered when the pain eased. "It's time. My water broke."

Keary stared at her blinking. She knew he must be in shock. A smack at his bare chest left a red hand print, but he snapped out of it. He jumped into action. "Your bag. Where is it?" Zacari almost laughed when he darted to the kitchen door and then ran back to her. He would have run off again if she didn't grab his hand. Another contraction hit. She crunched his fingers and screeched.

To his credit, Keary only winced, freed his hand, and then whipped her into his arms. When they made it out to the living room, he'd finally remembered where he left her bag. By the front door of course, that is when he wasn't packing and repacking it to be sure she had everything. Within a few minutes, they were speeding down the empty streets of Chicago toward the hospital.

While he drove, Keary dialed on his cell phone. He spoke with Zacari's doctor to be sure she would meet them at the hospital, and then he called his father. "Jack, it's time. Yes, okay, I'll see you and mom later today. Thanks."

He snapped the phone closed and reached for her hand. "Breathe, baby, just like we learned. I'm here for you. If you want to yell at me and call me names, it's fine. I understand."

Despite her weariness, Zacari managed a chuckle. "Trust me, I've already called you a few choice words in my mind, but why would you say that?"

"I read it."

She held up a hand. "Say no more. You've read more than I have on birthing babies. Let's just be quiet, because I'm feeling really grouchy right about now." Keary nodded and fell silent, but he didn't let go of her hand even when she squeezed the mess out of it. In his normal supportive way, he cast her encouraging looks and demonstrated now and then with his own breathing how she should. Zacari dug the nails of her other hand into her palm to keep from slapping him.

At the hospital, everything whipped into a frenzy. Zacari was wheeled to a birthing room with a million instruments and seemingly as many staff. "Drugs," Zacari shouted.

Keary's eyes widened. "We said we were doing this naturally for the baby's sake."

"What's this *we*?" she screeched. "Damn it, I'm in pain! Get me drugs!"

A nurse zipped in front of Keary to help her, and soon with everyone coming and going and instructing her on what to do, she lost sight of Keary. A few minutes later, her doctor arrived, and after a brief exam, determined that Zacari might not be ready to deliver for a few hours. Zacari sobbed.

The wait for the anesthesiologist was excruciating, and Zacari bit everyone's head off. Keary approached only long enough to get an angry glare and a blast of curses before he moved back. Zacari cried through hours of labor, and the epidural came only in time to be pointless because she was ready to give birth. By then Jack and Claudia were there, and Claudia breezed in after getting cleaned up and into scrubs.

The calm sweet woman wasn't intimidated in the least by Zacari's screams or angry words. She gripped Zacari's hand and stayed close. "You can spin your head around three sixty, honey, I'm staying."

Fresh tears spilled down Zacari's cheeks. "Thank you. I'm so sorry. Tell Keary I'm sorry. I'm horrible."

"She's just exhausted," a nurse commented about Zacari's sudden switch in attitude.

"I know," Claudia said. "I've got tough skin. And don't you worry, honey," she whispered in Zacari's ear. "He's never left the room. He understands."

When Zacari thought her son might be tearing through her back with each contraction, at last Keary O'Connor Junior came into the world with wide open eyes and a head full of hair. Claudia stepped back and relinquished Zacari's hand while Keary moved in close. His big strong hands shook when he touched their son's head, and he stroked the silky black curls. "He's amazing."

"Isn't he beautiful?" Zacari knew she must look a mess after that ordeal, but right now she didn't care. She drew her little one close to her chest and kissed his cheek. Keary's hand slipped into hers, and her heart swelled. For a second in time, they were like a real family.

"He is beautiful," Keary murmured, "just like you." He kissed her lips, and everyone in the room melted away, except her, Keary, and their son. But Zacari was tired out of her mind. Her lids were heavy, and although she didn't mean to, she kept falling asleep. Gently, Keary took the baby into his arms. She thought he would be afraid to hold something so tiny and fragile in his huge hands, but Keary was a natural. She wouldn't have put it past him to have studied books on the proper way to hold an infant.

While Keary sat rocking his son, Zacari watched him. She fell asleep over and over, but forced herself to wake up. The sight of them together was more than she'd ever dreamed. How mean she'd been to Keary over the last few months when he'd been nothing but good to her. He had been patient and kind. Countless times, he'd run out at a moment's notice to get her whatever she craved.

"You deserve so much more," she told him in a voice thickened by sleep.

He glanced up. "Hm? What do you mean?"

"You deserve more than me. I know you've been by me for JR, but you should have someone that you love in your life. I have no doubt whoever she is, she'll love you. That's not even an issue."

A myriad of emotions flickered over Keary's face,

including confusion, and then understanding dawned. He stood up. A nurse walked into the room before he could say anything. "I need to take him for tests if that's okay, Mommy and Daddy?"

Keary hesitated and then placed the baby in the basinet the hospital had supplied. He looked like he might follow them out, but then he turned back to Zacari. All emotion left his face, and although he seemed pleasant enough, she had the feeling he was angry. "So you're saying we're done. You don't need me anymore? He is my son too, Zacari, or had you forgotten?"

"Oh come on, Keary." She sighed and pulled to sit up. From the waist down, she was still numb. Her thighs felt like someone had tossed a heated blanket over them. "You know I haven't forgotten. Neither am I trying to insinuate that I don't want you in JR's life."

"Have we decided on calling him JR?"

"It's weird to call you both Keary without some kind of variation."

"Agreed."

"Anyway," she continued, "I'm just saying I see what you did for me, and I'm thankful, but you don't have to do anymore. Now you can concentrate on the baby and leave me out of it. I don't want to stand in the way of your happiness."

"Come off of it, Zacari," he snapped.

She gasped at his tone. She'd never seen him like this, even when he claimed he was grumpy when he hadn't had his morning coffee. She'd never seen evidence of that.

"We both know you are still insecure about your past. I've worked my ass off to show you how special you are, but none of it makes any difference." He ran a hand through his hair and rubbed his bloodshot eyes. "We've been up for more than twelve hours after only sleeping about three. This isn't the time to have this conversation. Neither of us is in the best mental state."

Too late, he had pissed her off. "I'm insecure? Pardon me for not falling at your feet because you spent a little money on me and our son. Excuse me for not kissing your toes when you tell me we should get married without any love!" Something flashed in his eyes, but she kept ranting. "You're right, I am insecure. Why should I think that all of a sudden because I got pregnant when I didn't mean to, some rich, sexy man is going to hand over my happily-ever-after. I live in reality. You love JR. I see that, and no one's going to take that away from you, so you can back off of *me*!"

They both stood there staring at each other, breathing hard in their anger. Keary's eyes were narrowed, his jaw tightened, and his hands bunched into fists in his pockets. He didn't move one muscle for a long time. Finally, he spoke in a low, calm voice, so low, she at first didn't think she heard right.

"You don't have to worry about me anymore, Zacari. I'm sick and tired of trying to get past your defenses. I will see you in court for joint custody."

Chapter Twelve

Keary tapped on his steering wheel as he glanced up at Zacari's apartment building. This tenuous truce they had was not working for him. Every time he walked into her place, all he wanted to do was take Zacari into his arms and prove to her that he loved her. Yeah, he'd come to that solid conclusion after he'd made his bold statement that he would see her in court. One night spent away from Zacari told him he needed her. No, that he loved her, and visiting would not work long term for him.

Of course in his anger, he had mentioned the situation to Jack, which only complicated matters. Now, Zacari thought he had already filed papers in court since his lawyer had been in contact with her to find out the name of Zacari's lawyer. On top of that, the man had overstepped his bounds and mentioned a paternity test to Zacari. Keary had fired him, but he hadn't gotten a chance to speak to Zacari to clear matters yet.

Now was that time. He sighed and slipped out of his car. How the hell the situation turned this ugly, he didn't know. When the doorbell resounded through her apartment, he wished he could take it back and just go home. Too late, he heard her coming to answer.

The door opened, and Keary felt a punch in his stomach. Zacari had been crying. Without thinking, he raised his hand to cup her cheek. "Baby." He lowered his head to kiss her but caught himself and drew back. She'd been willing a moment before but then averted her gaze.

"I'm not the one, Keary. You can come in so we can talk, but please keep your hands to yourself."

Keary heard the sadness. He wracked his mind to figure out a way to fix the situation. "Zacari, what my lawyer said to you was wrong. He jumped ahead of me."

"Ahead of you," she repeated. "Meaning you were planning to demand a paternity test, but you didn't mean for him to say anything just yet."

"No, that's not what I meant. Look can we not argue?" She turned and flounced away a few steps. He caught her arm and spun her to face him. She struggled, but he forced her to stand still and listen to him. "I'm not filing for custody, and I'm not asking for a paternity test."

She went still, eyes wide. "What did you say?"

"You heard me." He led her over to the couch and pulled her down beside him.

Zacari fiddled with her hands not meeting his gaze. "I was talking with Claudia, and she said Jack had—"

"Stop."

She blinked up at him.

"I'm not interested in what my mom or Jack said. I made the mistake of mentioning our argument to him, and he had his own opinions about what I should and shouldn't do. I told him then that this was not his business. You and I will decide what's best for JR, no one else. So, I get it, you don't want to marry me. That's fine."

"I—"

He put a finger over her lips. "We will work this out as two civilized adults, two parents who love their son very much and will fight hard to be sure he has all he needs from both of us."

What Keary hated most of all about this situation was coming to the realization that Zacari didn't love him and probably never would. He could show her all the kindness in the world, but she would see it as an extension of his love for JR, nothing more. He'd accepted it, but it didn't change how he felt about her or how hard life would be seeing her every day and not being able to hold her.

"Do we have a deal?" he asked when she said nothing.

"Yes, we do."

He forced a smile while turning away from her. "Now, how about a break? I want to see my son."

For the rest of the afternoon, they sat talking about JR. Keary found plenty of times they could have had a disagreement, like Zacari wanting to rush back to work after her six week checkup and him not wanting her to work at all. But he knew she was independent, and it had taken a lot for her to allow him and his family to purchase the things they did for the baby. He'd gotten her to agree to most of it by saying didn't he have a right to care for his son the way he knew how? Zacari had backed down, and now she never protested when he bought a new item for the baby.

He rocked his son in the crook of his arm, pride swelling his chest that he had been a part of creating him.

One day, he would teach JR to play ball, and he would advise him about girls. Keary bit off a bitter laugh. Well, hopefully by that time he'd get them himself.

"I respect your decision," he told Zacari. "And can I request that you make it at least another month?" Relief flooded him at seeing the weary sadness ease around her eyes, but unless he was mistaken, something still bothered her.

She moved over to the couch where he sat and let the baby grasp her fingers. Desire crept through Keary's system when her breast bumped against his arm. He should not be feeling this while holding his son, but he hadn't been with Zacari in a while, and he craved her. Last night using his hand hadn't eased the need one bit. His mind had been consumed with thoughts of Zacari. Should he try to seduce her? They could be lovers and nothing more. Their passion had been real.

No, she should have the right to feel what she wanted to and make decisions with a clear head. If she didn't want to be with him as his wife, he needed to accept it.

"Okay, one more month. I can stay home as long as Jeb is okay with it," she said.

"I'm sure he'll be fine with it."

She smirked. "Meaning you're going to *tell* him he's fine with it."

When the baby began to fuss, he handed him to Zacari. Keary watched in fascination as she undid her blouse, lowered a bra flap over her breast, and began to feed him. Ashamed that he was jealous of his own son, he looked away, but he felt Zacari's eyes on him. She could have moved her thigh when it brushed his, but she didn't. The woman had to know how she tormented him.

"I am not abusing my position," he told her for something to distract him from her body. "Company policy allows for extra maternity leave for mothers."

"Oh."

When she finished feeding the baby, she handed him back to Keary. He tossed a cloth diaper over his shoulder and rested his son against him before patting his back. When that task was done, from habit, Keary checked his son's diaper and then straightened his clothes.

"You're a good daddy," she said, laughing softly.

"That comes as a surprise?"

She shook her head. "No, I knew you would be."

Her words took him by surprise. "How did you know?"

"Because you're a good man, so gentle and patient."

Then why couldn't I make you fall in love with me?

Her gaze dropped to her fingers which were clutched together in her lap. "I was thinking that you might want to go with me to his doctor's appointment tomorrow. And then maybe we could have lunch together."

Keary was shocked into silence. She wanted him with her? She'd not mentioned it before. Of course she knew he wanted to spend every free minute being involved in his son's upbringing but to invite him to dinner was an extra step. Keary searched Zacari's face for a clue as to how she felt, but he could gather nothing. Before their big fight, she'd been open and easy to read, at least most of the time.

"Well?" she prodded. "If you don't want to, I understand."

"No, I do," he hurried to say. "I just wasn't expecting the invite. A minute ago, we were at each other's throats.

Granted much of it was misunderstanding and frustration on my part. I apologize for upsetting you, Zacari. That's the last thing I want."

So she wouldn't feel he was pushing again for something she wasn't willing for or comfortable with, he added, "I just want us to be friends and share in raising JR. I know we can do that without any outside interference. We did okay while you were pregnant."

A flicker of disappointment crossed Zacari's face confusing him again, but then she schooled her features into the sweet smile he loved. "You're right. We're going to be the best parents any child has ever had. Especially with you reading a library of parent help books."

She burst out laughing, and he joined her. "Hey, don't knock the reading. It will come in handy one day. I promise you."

"Whatever, Dr. Spock." She stood up, and he followed her to JR's room. Keary wasn't fooled by Zacari's digs at his reading. The fact that she knew Dr. Spock was probably the most well-known pediatrician in the world said she'd looked into the subject herself.

At his son's crib, Keary laid the baby down, and Zacari tucked him under a light blanket. Keary straightened and glanced around the room while Zacari wound up the mobile. They'd done the deco in the room together having picked out what they liked from a home décor magazine. Of course, that had been the easy part. The hard part was getting Zacari to agree to move to a two bedroom apartment and allowing him to pick up the extra cost in rent. It turned out that she loved the place, so the battle was well-won.

"What will you do with the rest of your day?" he asked.

She shrugged. "Nothing planned. I'm always so sleepy. I feel like I haven't had a full night's rest in years."

"If you like, I can come by later and watch JR while you get some extra sleep."

He thought she'd refuse, but her face brightened, and she rested a hand on his arm. "Really? You'd do that?" He nodded. "Thanks, and I'm going to cook you something good, so don't eat before you come."

Desire wound through him at her touch. He took a step closer but then realized it and backed off. "Thank you. You don't have to."

"I want to. Eight. Be on time," she teased, "or it will get cold."

"Then I'll be here. I look forward to it."

Keary left soon after and sat in his car for a few minutes just as he'd done when he arrived. That had been close. Her touching him made him want to scoop her into his arms and claim her lips in a kiss. He looked down to find his cock hardened, tenting his pants. She was in no mood to have sex, and he shouldn't even be thinking about it. Ashamed of himself, he adjusted his erection and turned over the car engine. After throwing the stick into drive, he peeled from the curb. At least he could look forward to later. He'd soak up every minute in her presence and let it be enough.

Chapter Thirteen

Zacari flipped through her cookbook and chewed on her bottom lip. She'd made her decision when Keary told her he would not be going to court or ordering a paternity test. This man was wonderful. He'd taken care of her far above and beyond what any father needed to in order to be a part of his child's life. She had to admit to herself that he cared—maybe loved, maybe not, but Keary did care about *her*. Fears and doubts still swirled in her mind and heart, but damn it, she was going to beat them down and win him over.

That afternoon, Keary had looked like he could eat her up the way he stared at her. And she had not missed how hard he got when he stood too close to her. He'd been about to kiss her. She wanted it because she loved and missed him, but her body wasn't quite ready for sex. Either way, Keary was the one, and she planned to do all in her power to show him that he hadn't been wrong in pursuing her. Hopefully, it wasn't too late.

"No," she muttered as she flipped pages, "it's not too late." She'd start with the meal tonight and work from there. Keary had been sweet and attentive. Now it was her turn to care for him and show him how much she appreciated and loved him.

She decided on steak tips in mushroom sauce, a side salad, and baked potato. For desert, she would make Keary's favorite, lemon meringue pie. She didn't prefer lemon flavor, but this was all about him. He'd be thrilled and stuffed to the gills if she could help it.

Between a couple naps and working at a reasonable pace, she got the meal together. The pie cooled in the refrigerator, and the food sat ready on the dining room table. Zacari had bathed and fed her son, and now all she needed was Keary. Just when she thought that, the bell rang. Her heart skipped a beat. Butterflies tormented her belly. One would think this was a first date and that they hadn't gone through thick and thin over the last few months. From that morning when she'd seen him until now, she'd chewed off her already short fingernails.

As she walked to the door, she scanned her figure and approved of the dress. Breastfeeding, watching what she ate, and light exercise had taken her stomach way down. Another twenty pounds and she'd be where she was pre-pregnancy. Okay, so she had a few stretch marks, but so did most women who'd been overweight or had a baby. Her breasts were heavier, and Keary seemed to like that. Her hips still curved nice, and despite the thicker thighs, her legs looked okay.

She opened the door. Keary's eyes widened. His attention strayed from her face, to her breasts, and then on down her body. "You're so beautiful." Reticence came over his expression as if he wanted to bite his tongue for admitting it. Zacari pretended it wasn't a big deal.

"Thanks. Come on in. The food's all ready, and you can eat whenever you like."

He followed her to the dining room. "Zacari, this is too much. You're supposed to be using this time to rest, not wear yourself out."

"Are you complaining about my food before you taste it?" She affected a pout, and he rushed to apologize.

Zacari suppressed a laugh and began dishing out food for him. She poured him a glass of red wine and herself a glass of water. A little later, she would have some caffeine free tea just to settle down before getting some rest.

"I made your favorite," she announced. "Lemon meringue pie."

Keary's fork paused half way to his mouth. "How did you know that?"

She laughed and tucked into her own small plate of food. "Claudia told me a while ago. She said she makes a habit of cooking all your favorites when you return from traveling out of the country for extended periods of time. I haven't been anywhere other than the Bahamas once when I was little, so I was kind of shocked when she said some places don't even have a decent hamburger."

He nodded. "Yeah, you know we have a non-profit division. I don't get involved with that part often, but sometimes I'm required to settle matters in a third world country. When that happens, the food isn't always… well…not up to our usual standards."

"Wow, I thought—"

He smirked. "You thought I was too uppity what with traveling around in limos, first class plane rides and such?"

She ducked her head and focused on chewing. "Yes. I guess I did. I'm sorry."

He reached across the table to grasp her hand. She guessed he didn't even think about it when his fingers linked with hers. She wasn't about to draw his attention to it. "Hey, I'm not perfect. I like the luxury. And when I do have to visit those countries, all I can think about is going home and enjoying what my money can provide. It's vain."

"Nothing wrong with that. I don't blame you."

"I feel like the more we do, the more there is to do." His eyes glazed over. "With the wealth we have accumulated, there's a responsibility to give back."

"What about taking care of home? Do y'all have a charity set up here to help Americans?" Keary looked guilty. This wasn't going the way she wanted. She had not meant to accuse him of falling down on the job. "Ah, forget I said that."

"No, if you have suggestions, I'll be glad to hear them."

Zacari looked up at him and found she couldn't turn away. Was he serious? Would he take what she said to heart and make some changes, help the poor people in the U.S.? "Are you going to do something, really?"

"Why not? There's a legitimate need isn't there? I don't know why we haven't contributed other than passing on a check to our favorite charity before now. What did you have in mind?"

"Uh, I don't know. I just said it."

Keary leaned toward her until his face was inches from hers. Her breath caught in her chest thinking that he would kiss her, but he didn't close the space between them. With gentle fingers, he caressed her cheek. It took everything inside of Zacari not to turn into his touch and close her eyes. Sure she wanted this, but if she moved in now, he might back off.

"This is your project," he told her. "You find out where there's a need and what C-O-C could do to make a change, and I will personally get it moving, hire staff, secure the facilities, whatever it takes."

She bit her lip, excitement brewing. This was like getting in on the ground floor of something worthwhile, work that changed lives. "What if I'd like a position myself in the new venture, I mean like a manager. I'm almost finished with school. I know I have the qualifications if not the experience. If you give me a chance, I can make it work."

He moved back, his expression closing a little. Zacari watched his eyes turn in the direction of the small teddy bear she'd left on the shelf behind them. Of course, Keary didn't want her to work. Just short of saying something pissy about him not having a problem why should she— she kept her lips closed. Keary wouldn't force her not to work by taking away her opportunities, but she knew where he stood. *And he knows where I stand.*

Would things always stand between them? She wouldn't fight him or upset him. There wasn't a need to yell and show him she was her own woman, independent and strong. He already knew all that, and yelling or even mentioning it would ruin their newfound peace. Zacari went back to eating, and so did Keary. Soon his plate was empty, and she gathered the dishes to place them in the kitchen sink. When she came back to the table, she brought him a piece of pie and sat in silence while he devoured it.

"This is delicious," he commented.

"Thank you."

"No, thank *you*. You didn't have to go to all this trouble."

"You're more than worth it." Right then she felt both frustration and love for Keary. She wanted to be with him, but maybe they were too different. As he had admitted, he loved his life of luxury, where everything was handed to him. Not that he didn't work his butt off. She saw that too.

No, she wouldn't go back on her decision to win him. Even a man who had the same background as she had wasn't as wonderful as Keary—not any that she'd met so far. And the fact remained that she loved him with all her heart.

When he stood up and gathered the dessert dishes, he focused on the bear once again. Zacari's stomach knotted at what he would say. "You know where I stand, and I know your position. Although everything inside of me wants to demand that you not work and take care of JR full time, it's not fair of me to ask that of you.

"I can remember back to five years old when I lost my mother. I can see a scene in my mind of my father holding Karen and me clutching his pants leg while we stood over my mother's bed. She'd never been strong physically, and having Karen had taken a lot out of her. She never recovered after giving birth the second time. The day she died my father wept. That was the only time I ever saw Jack cry. Afterward we were raised by a series of nannies until Jack had had enough. One day he stood Karen and I in front of him and told us he was going to find us a mother who would care for us one hundred percent of the time. It took seven months."

"Claudia?" Zacari asked.

He nodded. "She is the best mother a man can have, and you are the best mother for JR. I hate the thought of someone else caring for him, but I do understand your position."

Zacari could not believe how guilty she felt. Keary hadn't said the nannies had been mean to him and his sister, but the instability of it, the substitution of not having their mother. Everyone these days sent their children to daycare, and plenty of people turned out great. Many, she figured, would have loved to be the one to do it if they could. She had the opportunity because of Keary's money, but for real she'd go psycho trapped in the house all day every day.

Zacari's brain hurt thinking about it all, and weariness after a long day descended on her. She covered her mouth on a yawn. Keary moved to her and rested his hands on her hips. "Bedtime," he said with insistence.

"But I…"

"Uh-uhn, we had an agreement. You're not backing out of it."

She sighed and leaned into him as he led her toward her bedroom. Backing out required energy. She had none. "I guess you're right." She yawned again. "Milk's in the refrigerator. If you run out, just wake me up."

"Twenty-four seven supply, huh?" His interested gaze flickered to her breasts. Zacari's blood heated up, but another yawn took hold of her. Keary ignored protests while he lifted her into his arms and set her gently on the bed. She didn't fight him when he began unbuttoning the front of her dress. Breath trapped in her chest, Zacari tried not to let on how turned on she was.

Keary didn't have the same qualms, it seemed. His eyes never left her body as he began uncovering more skin, and when he reached down to remove her shoes, she caught a glimpse of the bulge in his pants. Her mouth watered. Her fingers itched to reach out and stroke him. How she missed his rigid hardness, his length, and the way his cock twitched with just a look from her or a word. Trusting him a lot more than she used to, Zacari figured he'd been without sex for a while. Five weeks slipped by since the last time they were together.

Shed of her dress, she kept her bra and panties on. Keary tugged the covers back and waited until she was beneath them before he tucked her in. Sitting on the side of the bed, he bent over her. Neither of them spoke a word as they looked into each other's eyes. Zacari took a chance and let all her feelings for him shine through her eyes. Keary seemed startled and then disbelieving. He opened his mouth to say something, but then JR whined in the other room.

Keary ran the back of his fingers over her cheek. "Get some rest. I'll take care of everything, and I'll be here in the morning when you wake up."

As he turned away and strolled to the door, her heart sank. She thought he'd seen her real feelings, how she loved him, but maybe he didn't believe it. Not after she had kept telling him no and pushing him away. The door closed while Zacari cried herself to sleep.

Chapter Fourteen

"Claudia, thank you for watching him," Zacari said. "I can't believe you flew all the way here to baby-sit."

Claudia waved her hand as she took JR into her arms. "Are you kidding? I'd go to the moon for my little grandson, and it's been two weeks since I've seen him. He is my world." She rolled her eyes. "Don't tell Jack that of course."

Zacari laughed. "I won't, but trust me he acts all distant and annoyed that Keary didn't do what he wanted with me and the baby, but I've caught him doing the baby talk. I know he loves JR just as much as we do."

"You're right. He's a doting granddad. So what are you planning?"

She blushed and busied her hands with her dress. She'd lost the extra weight, but it had been a while since she'd worn anything so tight and short. Keary hadn't stopped looking like he wanted to eat her over the last three months, so she figured he would like it. "Tonight, I'm going to show Keary what he means to me. I rented a limo and made reservations at a great restaurant."

Claudia whistled. "Nice, but why did you rent a car? Keary could have arranged for one for you and charged it to the company."

"That's the point. This is what I'm doing for him. I have to pay for it. Everything I planned is expensive as hell, but since he's still footing most of my bills, I figure I can swing the cost." She grinned. "I'm going to show him the time of his life."

"Oh, TMI, honey, TMI! Let me stop you right there." Claudia turned toward the kitchen, apparently to ready a bottle. "You have a great time." She paused in the kitchen doorway and looked back at Zacari. "I hope tonight he realizes just how much you love him."

"I—"

"Good night." Claudia disappeared through the door before Zacari could find a response.

They had discussed her feelings for Keary, and Claudia had said Jack knew how she felt too, but that didn't stop the mere mention of it from embarrassing the hell out of her. After all tonight she was taking a chance. Keary wanted her, but he might not be willing to go back to a closer relationship. He might have written her off. Now that he had picked up his working schedule again and she saw him less often, for all she knew he could be dating another woman.

Pain squeezed her heart at just the thought. Knowing Keary, she believed he would tell her if he was, but she felt no less afraid of it. Zacari gathered her purse and a wrap. She took a deep breath and walked out the front door. In the parking lot, the limo waited, and when the driver opened her door, she slid inside.

"You have the address where we're picking up my

friend?" she asked him before he closed the door.

The man nodded. "Yes, ma'am. We'll be there in a jiffy."

"Thanks."

She settled back against the soft cushions and closed her eyes. As soon as she did, her phone began to ring. Fishing it from her purse, she hoped it wasn't Keary checking up on when she'd get there. Before she spoke with him, she needed a little more time to get her mind wrapped around what she would do. The caller ID said Jack. Zacari's chest tightened all the more.

"Hello, Jack. Is anything wrong?"

"Does something have to be wrong for me to call the mother of my grandson?"

She frowned. Well, they sure didn't shoot the breeze on a regular basis. The man still seemed way out of her reach. She had traveled to his house once after that initial meeting, but it had been on her terms. After that, he and Claudia visited practically every week, but they stayed in a fancy hotel. If she had hoped to keep them at arm's length, she was mistaken. All three of them wanted into JR's life. She couldn't blame them. Her son was perfect, and he won every person's heart who looked into his aqua green eyes.

Just like his daddy's.

"No, it doesn't. I'm sorry. How are you?" she said.

"I'm fine. I hope you are as well and little Keary?"

She rolled her eyes. *"Little Keary."* Jack had refused to call JR by his nickname from day one. "He's doing great. I just left him with Claudia. He was sleeping."

"Good. I'll call her after I speak with you." He hesitated, and she knew something was coming. Jack wouldn't call just to ask how the baby was doing. Claudia was the one who did that, and Zacari had often heard her calling over her shoulder to Jack, telling him whatever news Zacari had to share about her son. When she was close to yelling for him to get on with whatever he had to say, Jack continued. "I wanted to say I think you're a good woman, and I know if Keary opens his eyes and make you his wife, I support his decision one hundred percent."

Zacari's jaw dropped. "Come again? I mean...thank you."

"Claudia told me about your special night tonight. I'm aware that my son loves you and you love him. The two of you have been pussyfooting around for a few months, which is very unlike Keary. He usually pursues what he wants without hesitation. But I know that the situation you two found yourselves in was different. I stayed out of it so he could decide on his own."

This was you staying out of it? Advising him to get a paternity test?

"Thank you. I appreciate you telling me that," she responded. "I hope you're right about Keary loving me, and that with all that's come between us, it's not too late to fix our relationship."

"Your troubles are minor," he assured her. "There's just you, him, and your son. You can build things from there."

Tears filled her eyes. She couldn't believe Jack was being this kind, but then he'd never really been mean to her. Just not that encouraging with hers and Keary's relationship.

"If you ever need anything—and I do mean anything,

Zacari—do not hesitate to come to me. You understand?"

She sniffed, blinking so she wouldn't ruin her makeup. "Yes, sir. Thank you, Jack. Thank you so much."

They chatted a little while longer about her plans for the evening, and then Jack said he couldn't wait for Claudia to tell him about little Keary. The excitement in his voice made her smile. Up until now she had been dreading their first Christmas together with the baby because Jack had insisted they spend it in New York. Now, she looked forward to it.

At Keary's apartment, Zacari stepped out of the limo. They'd driven into the underground garage, and a bank of elevators stood to their right. She knew only one went up to the penthouse suite were Keary lived when he was in Chicago. She'd been there a few times. Waiting to reach his floor, she shook herself trying to dislodge the nervousness, but it wasn't working. When the bell dinged on his floor, she jumped. The doors slid open, and there he was, sexy as hell dressed in a black suit that fit his bulky muscled build to perfection.

Zacari got lost in his eyes from the moment she made contact with her own. He put his hand out, and she placed hers in his. Desire took hold, and she knew her panties were on their way to being ruined. "Um…" she began.

"You look edible," he commented.

Yep, her panties were gone. "Thank you. So do you."

"Would you like to come in for a drink?" he offered.

"We can't. The reservations were hard to get with short notice, and I admit I mentioned the O'Connor name to secure our spot. I don't want to push it."

"Baby"—Since they'd stopped being lovers, he hardly ever called her baby, and she missed it—"you didn't have to do all this. I could have arranged things."

She tugged him into the elevator and pushed the button for the garage. "It's your birthday, and I know you'd just love to have taken charge of it all." She laughed. "It's probably eating you up not to have control. Don't worry. I've got this."

"Oh, I'm not worried. I trust you." His gaze lowered over her body, pausing at her breasts. The dress she wore was cut low showing some cleavage. Zacari still needed the extra protection since she was breastfeeding, but the bigger boobs looked hot. Or so she thought. From the hungry look in Keary's eyes, he must agree.

Deciding to start on her seduction, she ran her hands over her shoulders, skimming the swell of her breasts. When she was beneath them, she gave them a gentle squeeze and then continued down to her belly. Just above her pussy, she paused again. "Do you like this dress?" For good measure she thrust out a bare thigh.

Keary put a finger where her hand was. The electricity that sparked between them from the barest touch made her lips part, and she caught her breath. He ran his finger over her belly, teasing the slight indentation at her navel.

"That dress is too much and too little at the same time."

"Oh?"

He narrowed his eyes focusing on her legs. "So much skin uncovered, yet not enough."

Zacari resisted pushing the emergency stop button and jumping him right there. Turning away, she stepped ahead of him and waited for the doors to open. Keary rested his hands at her waist as he stood behind her. His breath tickled the top of her head.

"One would never believe you'd had a baby three months ago," he said.

She walked forward and glanced over her shoulder at him. His stare was glued to her ass. "I know right?" Zacari added a bit more sway in her hips than necessary. Keary followed, she guessed, led by his rigid cock.

Later, over their delicious meal, Zacari slipped her foot out of her shoe and ran it along Keary's leg under the table. "So what do you think about us picking up where we left off? I mean as lovers."

Although she'd been teasing him all night what with leaning over the table to give him a better view of her breasts, reaching across the table to touch him, and complimenting him, Keary seemed hesitant.

"I'm not sure that's good for either of us."

Her eyes widened. She sat down the glass of juice she'd been sipping from. How she'd wanted wine, but the alcohol would get into her milk and affect JR. She wasn't having that. Besides, Keary would skin her if she even thought about it. "What do you mean? It was okay before JR was born, and you even wanted more."

His focus never wavered from her face, which made her shift around in her seat. "Yes, I did want more."

Zacari tangled her fingers in the cloth napkin on her lap. "And now you don't."

"I didn't say that."

She sighed. "Say what you mean, Keary. You've always been upfront with me."

"Okay." He shrugged. "I'm not going to deny how much I want you. I could eat you up the way you look tonight. Trust me, it's taking all of my self-control not to touch you. The same goes for every other night when

I'm around you, including when you're in that hideous nightgown I hate."

She allowed a half smile.

"However, being your lover is not what I want."

Could he have been blunter? "Oh." She stared at the table, ready to run out of there because she'd made a fool of herself thinking she could seduce him into bed and everything would be fine. "Well, look, I had tickets to that movie you wanted to see, but if you prefer, you can take someone else. I understand."

"Damn it, Zacari, when are you going to open your eyes?" he growled.

Her temper flared. "I don't know what you're talking about. You just said you don't want me. I'm supposed to continue this evening like no big deal? Come on, you know what I was doing, trying to seduce you."

"I don't want to be seduced...not really."

She balled up her napkin and threw it on the table. "Then what the hell do you want, because I don't get it? I don't know what I'm supposed to open my eyes to. You said you could eat me and that you've wanted to every time you've seen me, but you don't want to be my lover? What the hell, Keary? I think you need to—"

"I love you."

Her tumbling words stuttered to a halt at his announcement. Zacari sat there stunned. "Y-You said... you love me?"

He reached out and took her hands in his. "Baby, I don't want to *just* be your lover. I want so much more than that. If all you're offering me is access to your body, that's amazing and wonderful, but it's not enough. Zacari, I can't stand being away from you. I hate it when I don't hear your voice or see your face. Do you have any idea how tormenting it is for me when I'm away on business? I find every excuse to call at every opportunity."

She watched as he linked his fingers with hers, love and desire swelling within her. Sure, Claudia and Jack both told her Keary loved her, and she thought she'd seen it flash in his eyes countless times, but to hear him utter those words. It seemed too much to take in or even to believe. "You never said," she whispered.

"I didn't think you'd believe me or accept it," he said. "Remember when I asked you to be my wife, you thought it was for JR's sake. And for the most part it was, until I realized just how much I cared about you. I think it began from that first night. I couldn't get you out of my head, and it wasn't just the sex."

"You were going to start something with Debbie, which I understand because—"

"No."

She looked up at him.

"Before I realized what was in my heart, I started up with her, but the whole time, I kept thinking of you. She was interesting to talk to, but we connected on an intellectual level, not personal."

"We're only connected on the personal. I can never match what she knows business-wise. I mean we're in the beginning stages of starting your charity in the U.S., but there's so much I don't know. You've seen that. And we still don't agree about me going back to work. You convinced me to delay longer and take a short leave until JR is six months old."

"Did I convince you, or did you want it too? Admit it; you're having trouble leaving him."

He was right. Every time they talked about her going back to work, she let Keary talk her into waiting longer. She couldn't blame him. Leaving JR hurt like hell. The pain was probably the same for every mother, and because Keary could afford to support her and the baby, she had an excuse to indulge it. Still, she felt guilty and was afraid that she'd lose something of herself if she depended too much too long on Keary.

"You're right," she said. "I don't want to leave him. I wish there was a way I could interact with others more and stimulate my brain while not leaving him."

"If I say there is, then what?"

She blinked at him. "Tell me."

"The charity, remember? We discussed helping young mothers. What if we go with some type of training facility that will encourage mothers to bring their babies in while they're learning new skills to give them better opportunities in life? There would be caregivers there to assist and a separate section for the babies so the learning isn't interrupted. If you get involved in that project, you can take JR with you. Although I would request that the hours not be full time for you. Is that reasonable?"

She shrieked. "Are you kidding? That is awesome. I can't wait to talk more about it and hash out the details. What kind of timeline are you considering?"

He dropped his voice low and raised her hand to kiss it. "I'd rather discuss whether you think it's possible for you to love me in time."

Zacari's heart thundered in her chest. Excitement took control so much that she didn't care whether she ruined her makeup crying. She swiped at the tears streaming down her face. "I already love you, Keary. I love you with all my heart, and there is no other man on this planet that I trust more. I want to spend my life showing you just how wonderful I think you are."

Keary didn't say a word. He wiped his mouth and raised his hand to signal the waiter. When the man came over, Keary requested the check and pulled his wallet out.

"I was going to handle that," she told him.

He signed his signature and left a sizable tip before standing up. "Come on, baby. I want you alone now."

His eyes practically glowed with a mixture of lust and love. Zacari's body heated up, and she tumbled behind him as he rushed them out the door. At first she thought the limo would take a while, but then after Keary called for it, five minutes later the vehicle slid to a smooth stop in front of them.

Keary had her tucked in and commanded the man behind the wheel to just drive. He turned back to her, mischievousness now reflected in his eyes. "We started out in the limo, we will finish here. Or at least this chapter."

"Oh," was all she could manage.

He pulled her onto his lap and rested his forehead against hers. "Zacari, I don't have a ring with me since I couldn't imagine this night would turn out like this. But I promise you, we will rectify that in the morning."

"A ring?" She knew what he was getting at, and her stomach was in knots. She wanted to hear him say it. This time, she'd know better than to deny him.

"You would make me the happiest man on earth if you would agree to be my wife." He grasped her face on both sides and lifted her head to kiss her. Zacari melted against him, loving the feel of his tongue gliding over her lips. She closed her eyes, drinking him in. When he drew back, she shuddered. "Zacari, you are my life. Please say yes."

"Yes, definitely yes, Keary. I love you so much."

He devoured her mouth while ripping at her dress. The delicate material tore away to reveal her bra. Keary broke their kiss to taste her skin from her throat to her chest and lower to her breast. He yanked her bra down so he could glide his wet tongue across her nipple and take it into his mouth. Zacari threw her head back, arching into his touch. She gripped his shoulders and pulled him closer.

"Oh, Keary, that's so good. The other one," she begged. "Take the other one.

He uncovered her other nipple but paused to look into her eyes. "What would you like me to do, baby?"

"Suck it," she moaned. "It aches for your mouth."

He laved her tight nipple and ran his teeth lightly over its surface. With a gentle kiss, he sent her into orbit. "Does any other part of your beautiful body need my mouth?"

"Yes, all of me."

"I aim to please." He reached beneath the dress bunched at her waist and pulled her panties to one side. When he tested her opening, she shuddered. Her pussy was drenched, and she curled her fingers around his wrist to pull him closer. Keary uttered a low whistle. "Mm, is this for me, baby?"

"Of course."

"And do you want me to eat you?"

"Yes!"

He tugged at her clit between two fingers and pinched while bringing his mouth back to her nipple. Zacari had trouble not screaming out her pleasure when he stroked her pussy from front to back and then penetrated her with two fingers. He coated his digits to the hilt and then leaned back to let her watch him lick her come from them.

"Take off your panties," he commanded.

She climbed off his lap and quickly shed the rest of her clothing and shoes. Expecting Keary to eat her pussy while she lay on her back, she was about to get into position, but he stopped her.

"No, on your knees."

"But I thought…"

"Did you not just tell me you trust me more than anyone?" He squeezed her now bare ass. "Do as I tell you. Face away from me on your knees."

Zacari didn't even want to question him further. Whatever he planned, she was all for it. If he needed to get his cock inside her now, whatever. She knew he would make sure she'd come and come hard. Keary wouldn't stop there either. The man could last a while after he came the first time, and he'd bring her to multiple orgasms. Of that, she had no doubt.

She flipped over and turned so her back was to him, and she stretched across the limo's backseat on her knees, ass in the air. Keary moaned and ran a hand over her ass and down the outside of her legs. He came up between her thighs, teased the outer rim of her pussy, and then pushed his fingers inside. Zacari arched into his touch, whining and wanting more.

When she felt the first flicker from his tongue, it

shocked her. Keary was going to eat her out from behind. He had to push her ass cheeks apart and nuzzle past her anus to get to her pussy, but he licked with relish. All the strength left her so that the upper part of her body collapsed. Keary took hold of her hips and forced her back to his mouth. He sucked hard on her clit. She cried out, but he didn't stay there. He glided the tip of his tongue over her folds, lapped up all her juices before dipping deeper to get more.

Zacari's muscles quivered. She whined in pleasure every time he delved inside of her, but he didn't neglect her button for a second. Every now and then, he'd return to her clit and suck hard enough to ache, but so good that she felt her orgasm building. She wriggled with his every touch and reached between her legs to tease herself when he concentrated on eating her.

"Make me come, Keary. I need it."

"I will, baby, hold on. You are mine now, and I *will* satisfy you." He kissed her clit and feathered more along her folds and back to her anus. Keary pushed her fingers away and used his own hand to stroke her while his tongue teased the edges of her anus.

"Keary," she shouted, unable to hold back another second. Her orgasm screamed through her body, tightening her muscles and making her pussy weep and clench. She gripped the door's handrail for dear life as she shook and cried through her release. When the bliss-filled waves eased, Keary sat up and yanked open his pants.

She watched over her shoulder while he pulled his cock free of his boxers. His desire was so out of control, he didn't wait to shove out of his clothes, but he grasped her at the hips and jerked her backward. Zacari gasped when Keary pushed his cock deep into her channel. Her lover could not be bigger and yet he felt like it. Her walls strained around him, sucking him in, clenching to keep him there. But Keary wasn't hearing that. Almost immediately, he began a fast pump in and out.

He leaned down and wrapped an arm around her waist, then hoisted her toward him. At the same time, he dropped into the seat, and Zacari was on his lap facing away from him. His cock was buried so far inside of her, she thought she would burst, but he didn't let up. He pulled her head back to his shoulder while lifting her up and letting her fall down his cock. Zacari arched to get more room for his entry. Keary held her in a steel grip she couldn't escape from if she wanted.

"Do you know how long I've wanted this?" he demanded in her ear. "How much I've needed it, hell needed *you*?"

"I'm sorry, Keary."

He pumped faster. She struggled to catch her breath. Impossibly, she was ready to come again, but Keary's movements seemed all about his climax. She wanted to give it to him, to satisfy him. His roughness excited her and felt amazing if not a tad painful. Keary twisted her so he could gain access to her breasts. When he sucked her nipple and pounded her pussy, Zacari shouted through another orgasm. But this time, Keary was right along with her. Seconds after she jerked in a powerful climax, his hot seed filled her pussy. Zacari moaned with every sensation until it eased, and she collapsed on Keary's chest.

"I'm not done," he announced, and when he knocked

on the glass separating them from their driver, Zacari watched in awe and anticipation. "Take me home," he commanded of the driver. The man grunted a response, and the car soon made a U-turn on the street they traveled along.

Keary didn't allow Zacari to move from his lap until they arrived at his apartment. He hastily yanked Zacari's dress down around her hips to cover her bare pussy and behind, but the top was ruined. He slipped out of his suit jacket to wrap it around her shoulders. Zacari held the coat closed and followed Keary from the underground parking lot to the bank of elevators. When they arrived at his floor, he reached out and took her shoes from her hand and relieved her of his jacket. "Take that off," he ordered, indicating her dress.

She stripped, and Keary did the same. He led her down the hall to his room. She stood in the doorway while he rummaged in a drawer. "What are you looking for?"

"On the bed. Now."

She gasped at his tone. Chills raced along her spine. This was a side to the man she'd never seen or heard. Keary had always been gentle with her, sweet and accommodating. All of a sudden, he took control to a whole new level, and she liked it. Curious to see where this was going, she obeyed and climbed onto his king size bed. She rearranged the pillows behind her and rested against the headboard. Keary turned around with something purple. When he drew closer, she realized what it was—silken rope. Her mouth formed a small *o*.

Keary climbed on the bed between her legs. "Are you opposed to this?"

"Are you nuts?" She bit her lip.

He didn't have to be told twice. While she watched in fascination, he began tying her wrists to the bed posts. The bonds were tight but not painful. No man had ever done this to her, and she found she liked it. To give up all control to him, to trust him not to hurt her more than she could bear was a heady feeling.

When he was done, Keary stroked her cheek and stared into her eyes. "There's so much I want to show you and experience with you, Zacari. Your body drives me insane, and all I can think about is having you and tasting you."

"I feel exactly the same," she whispered. Turning her head so that her mouth brushed his palm, she closed her eyes, luxuriating in the feel of him. Her heart thundered in her chest. Keary allowed her to kiss his hand for a while longer, and then he stood up and moved closer. He grasped her beneath the chin and lifted her head.

"Now, suck," he instructed.

She knew he was coated still with her juices, but the fact that he hovered over her head and that she couldn't get away turned her on. She wanted it, needed to have him in her mouth. Keary threaded his cock between her lips, and Zacari took every inch. He grasped the back of her head and pushed forward to pump against her face. At first his movements were slow and steady. He pushed his long, thick cock until it touched the back of her throat, and then he withdrew. He glided in, and then retracted.

When they had gotten a feel for how far he could go, Keary increased the pace. Slowly at first and then at amazing speed, he thrust into her mouth. The fear that any second he'd misjudge only drove them both higher.

Zacari reached between her legs and stroked her clit while Keary tangled his fingers in her hair. He grunted and swore. She knew by the sounds he made, he was going to come, but to her surprise, he stopped.

"Baby, you were close."

He shook his head. "Not yet." She sat still while he undid the ropes from the bed but kept them wound around her wrists. He brought the two pieces together in one hand. "On your belly."

She obeyed and flipped to face down. Keary put a pillow beneath her hips and then kneed her legs apart. He smacked her butt cheek, and she cried out. "That's for rubbing your clit when that's for me to do," he ground out.

She moaned. Keary smacked her ass again, and Zacari felt another orgasm coming on. While her lover rubbed away the pain, he wound the rope around his hand so that all the slack was taken up. He jerked her arms over her head. When she felt something that wasn't his hand at her anus, she stiffened.

"No, don't tense up. You'll like this," he told her. After coating the device in her flowing juices, Keary brought the thing around so she could see it. No more than four and a half inches and black with three tiers of bulbs, it grew wider from tip to base. She recognized it as a butt plug, which she'd seen on adult toy sites but never experienced. A shiver passed over her. "Do you want it?"

She pushed her ass in the air. "Yes."

"Yes, what?"

"Yes, Keary?"

He chuckled. "Yes, please."

She echoed his words, and then he pushed the small device into her rear entrance. First he worked the top in and rotated the plug a while until her muscles relaxed. Then bit by bit he pushed in the rest of it until her anus felt full. The sensation made her want to cry and moan at the same time. She pushed back against it and wriggled her hips.

With expert movements, Keary teased her. He leaned down and rained kisses along her back. His groans vibrated over her skin, amplifying her pleasure. Keary released her hands and sat back to drag her up onto his lap. Like it knew where it belonged, his cock brushed along her pussy and then eased inside with little guidance from him. All the while, he kept the plug moving, and Zacari was filled in both the front and the back.

As he pumped into her with his cock and thrust the plug in and out, she gripped the sheets in her hands. She cried out his name, pleading with him to let her come. Her orgasm built to the point of driving her insane. Zacari arched into Keary, pushing down hard. His cock was deeper than she remembered getting it, and all she wanted was to be consumed by him.

"Keary, it's so good. I can't get enough. I can't take it." Her words jumbled together, while her head spun at the overwhelming sensations.

His hand came down heavy on her, and he shoved her deep on his cock. Zacari screamed. Keary pounded fast and hard, calling out encouragement as he went. He didn't stop until together they shouted into the most potent orgasm Zacari had ever had.

Exhausted and unable to move afterward, Zacari lay still while Keary removed the plug and untied the rope. He shifted her into his arms and carried her to the bathroom. When he had turned on the shower and made sure the water was at a comfortable temperature, he helped her into it and gently washed her from head to toe. He cleaned himself while Zacari watched, and then they stepped together onto the mat at the side of the tub. He dried them both, and picked Zacari up to carry her back to the bed.

Once they were comfortable in each other's arms and the lights were off, Zacari nuzzled closer to Keary, blowing out a sigh of contentment. "Keary?"

He yawned. "Hm?"

"When can we do that again?"

He chuckled. "Baby, that was only the beginning. I have so much more to show you, and we can do it as often as you like."

"Is that a promise?"

"Of course."

She chewed her lip and considered something else that had been on her mind. "Keary?"

"Hm?"

"I was thinking JR would love a playmate."

Keary turned her in his arms, and she imagined the aqua green eyes had darkened as they usually did when her man was sexually excited. "Well in that case, there's no time like the present to start working on it."

"I couldn't agree more!"

About the Author

Tressie Lockwood has always loved books, and she enjoys writing about heroines who are overcoming the trials of life. She writes straight from her heart, reaching out to those who find it hard to be completely themselves no matter what anyone else thinks. She hopes her readers enjoy her short stories. Visit Tressie on the web at www.tresslock.webs.com.

Made in the USA
Lexington, KY
11 December 2010